THE TANGIER OPTION

**U.S. NAVY and OSS
OPERATION TORCH**

HAROLD MALT

THE TANGIER OPTION

U.S. NAVY and OSS
OPERATION TORCH

HAROLD MALT

Ethos Publishing, 4224 Spanish Trail Place
Pensacola, Florida, 32504

The Tangier Option: Copyright © 2009 by Harold Malt. All Rights reserved. No part of this publication may be reproduced, restored or transmitted in any form or by any means whatsoever.

ISBN: 978-0-9714692-3-5

Cover design and maps, Harold Malt
Cover production, Georgia Beliech
Cover photograph, F-4-F aircraft, courtesy National Archives

Ethos Publishing
4224 Spanish Trail Place, Pensacola, Florida 32504

AUTHOR'S NOTE

This book recreates the events surrounding espionage and Operation Torch in Tangier Morocco during the Second World War. More than seventy percent of it is documented fact. Although mention is made of political and military leaders within historical context of the period, it is stressed that this is a work of fiction and no reference is intended to any living or dead person.

ACKNOWLEDGEMENTS

Thanks to Thor Kuniholm, Director of the Tangier American Legation Museum (former Consulate) for access to archives containing espionage accounts by American participants, to Colonel Jack Kichler USA ret. (and MD) and Don Priest both of whom reviewed my work and provided suggestions, also to RADM Peter Booth who provided introduction to a Navy aircraft simulator, I offer sincere thanks.

For my wife Carol Malt with love

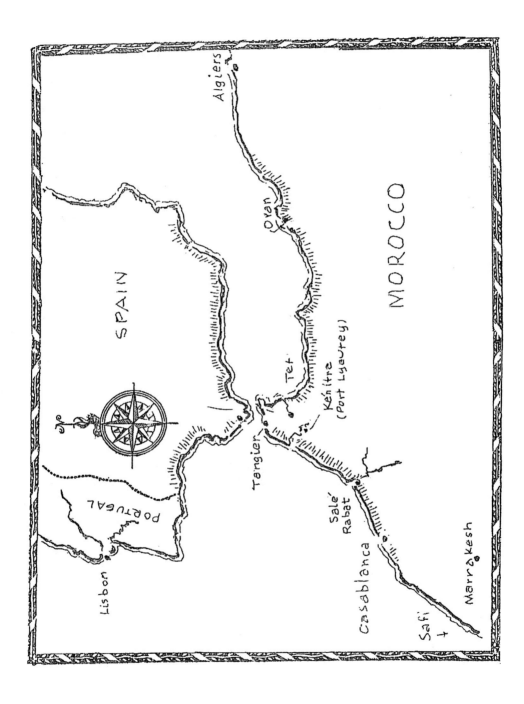

Chapter One

His turn would be next. He had worked hard to get here.

Peering through the windscreen, he knew this was the *big* one. Impatient, he glanced to his right at his instructor leaning on the carrier island's railing and watching him.

To get here, he had had several instructors starting in grueling Ground School with its many courses to master in seamanship, meteorology and aerodynamics. Though difficult, they were essential. Next came the moments of fear amidst hours of fun; five months of stalls, spins and aerobatics – learning to feel at home in the sky. Seeing stars above and scanning lights below during night cross-country navigation flights had been a lark. But practicing all those tail-hook landings at the Naval Air Station's Sherman Field in Pensacola, Florida was serious business. Jernigan became known as a 'good-stick.'

Now all he needed was this one landing at sea to become carrier qualified. Then would come his operations assignment. When offered the choice of three types of aircraft: fighter, scout dive-bomber or torpedo bomber, he had three times checked: 'fighter'. Way to go!

He always hoped for the Pacific fleet. It might give him a chance to say hello to his navy father sailing in that area.

The weather aloft reported as CAVU could not be better, although looking down at the Gulf of Mexico the white capped waves looked rough. This ship, the *USS Concord*, designated CV 2 when converted from battle cruiser to carrier, heaved and pitched.

Inside the carrier island and four levels up, this bucking worried Flight Ops Lt. Commander Harrison. Was it severe enough to cancel this last cadet's effort?

The carrier started a slow turn into the wind.

John Joseph Jernigan, known to classmates as JJ, flexed the fingers of his left hand that rested on three lever knob he had pushed forward – throttle, medium power; propeller pitch, low; fuel mixture, rich. The T-6 all-metal trainer built by North American Aviation vibrated, wanted to go. All he had to do was make this carrier take-off and landing. Wings of Gold would be his.

He made a third cockpit check: canopy hood open and slid back, flaps down, all instrument panel needles in the green, barometric pressure set. He breathed deeply when the earphones in the cloth headgear crackled.

"SNJ two four, wind fourteen knots gusting nineteen. Cleared for take-off."

The flight-deck officer gave him a thumbs-up. Jernigan looked right, nodded. Two deckhands yanked away chocks restraining the front wheels. His left hand jammed forward the power lever to its stop, his feet released pressure on rudder-pedal brakes. The 550 hp Pratt

& Whitney radial engine roaring at maximum power mashed him into the aluminum seat.

Staring down the wood planked deck, he moved the joystick between knees slightly forward – the tail rose . . . the aircraft drifted left. Pushing right rudder pedal to counter engine torque, he was off the deck in seconds and, with stick held back in his lap, climbing. No other aircraft were in the carrier's airspace. It was a hell of a feeling, his sensation of climbing high over water, into vast space.

Level and turning left into the downwind leg of a rectangular landing pattern, Jernigan throttled back to 125 knots. He glanced downward to adjust his position relative to the carrier. It wasn't there.

Where was it? At last sighting the carrier it seemed no bigger than his thumb. Well, that wasn't too swift. He'd flown too far out and too high. Jernigan cut power to lose altitude to 640 feet mean sea level. While checking his position and doing a landing cockpit check he began another descent. A warning light came on, then a loud buzz. He released the tail hook – the long rod of steel whose claw at the end would catch any one of three arresting wires raised slightly above deck level.

Turning and losing altitude while descending to 300 feet, he positioned himself astern the fast approaching deck. Now he focused eyes on the Landing Signal Officer. The LSO's two paddles were outstretched at arms length. Looking good . . . all on the money.

Except. Suddenly one paddle rose higher than the other. Oh-oh! Wind must have blown him toward the carrier's right side where soared the Operations Island. The LSO's paddles signaled 'wave-off'. He banked left, 'poured the coal to her' and with a forced grin plastered to his face, roared past the tall and massive superstructure. He wasn't worried.

Before taking his turn Jernigan had watched two classmates who also had been signaled to abort their landing. Nothing to it – just follow 'go around' procedure. He did likewise. Now, sighting the carrier, he performed the checklist, flew further out in order to have more time to get properly positioned for the approach.

At 250 feet MSL he was properly centered, dragging her in and this time losing altitude before reaching the deck. The LSO had his arms stretched downward signaling too low. Jernigan gave the trainer more power, still too low. He applied much more power – jammed the throttle forward – the nose shot up. Too high! Go around. Again.

No bravado grins this time as twenty-five feet high he roared the length of the deck. Watching him now were not only instructor and classmates, but also other officers on the carrier's Island.

The knuckles of his clenched throttle hand gleamed white but his right hand fingertips curled lightly around the joystick. Moving it one half-inch in any direction multiplied the change in aircraft attitude manifold times. His spine felt locked up tight. Beads of sweat formed, rolled down inside his goggles.

Take more time; settle down, he told himself. Yes, he was uptight, but disciplined too. Reviewing mistakes of the previous two attempts he made a choice. Instead of dragging her in for the final approach onto the pitching carrier, he would establish a constant glide slope and power setting, smack this beast onto the deck. That was it –

keep nose high, tail-hook down, snag the first cable, jerk to a stop. He definitely was not going to do another go-around.

Gray eyes ice cold, lips pressed tight, Jernigan turned inward to the carrier, adjusted airspeed to suit his constant angle of descent. He was in command of this airplane and he was telling what to do. Staring through the windscreen, approach was looking good. The carrier loomed larger, larger. LSO had paddles outstretched, motionless. Good. Almost there . . .

The carrier stern heaved up.

He was too low.

Should he pull the nose higher, or put her into the drink?

He decided an instant too late.

The airplane slammed into the ship's stern.

The propeller struck first, its two aluminum blades screeching, curling.

The landing gear sheared off, tumbled into the sea.

The trainer flipped end-over-end onto the deck, slid with its tail-hook pointing skyward.

"Damn," Jernigan muttered, hanging upside down in his parachute harness, blood dripping from a forehead cut. "I'm a washout. Wait until father hears about this."

Chapter Two

White House Oval Office
Sunday, December 7, 1941, 5:00 p.m.

In front of the curved ceiling-to-floor French windows overlooking the Rose garden, Franklin Delano Roosevelt leaned back in his swivel chair and asked Grace Tully, his private secretary: "Under 500 words?" He wanted this broadcast terse, every word stirring.

"Yes, Mr. President."

Roosevelt glanced at Harry Hopkins, trusted advisor seated alongside. Hopkins nodded in approval then said, "One suggestion."

Tired and pensive this bitter afternoon, FDR rubbed weary eyes. Always in bed by nine o'clock, he would not be this night.

"Write it down Grace."

Hopkins spoke to the secretary. "Next to last sentence, add this: 'With confidence in our armed forces . . . with the unbounded determination of our people, we will gain the inevitable victory . . . so help us God'."

Roosevelt motioned, "Use it, Grace. That will be all."

He inserted a cigarette in an ivory and ebony holder, snapped into flame a gold Ronson lighter and clenched the up-tilted holder between teeth. He watched curling streams of smoke until his secretary disappeared.

Hopkins moved the leather armchair a bit closer to the desk. He listened quietly to Roosevelt who mused in a melancholy voice: "Pearl Harbor. Couldn't be helped. Both our intelligence services focused on the Atlantic Ocean ignored the Pacific. General George Strong at Army G-2, Navy ONI too, both of them missed that boat."

Roosevelt jabbed the cigarette holder at Hopkins. "I am fed up with military intelligence rivalry and all their ambiguity. Army decodes and interprets a message one way. Navy wastes two months to decode, to analyze, then, can you believe, I get a different interpretation. Espionage is too fragmented, too self-serving. I've got too many people rowing this boat."

Roosevelt studied the cigarette ash, reflected and added. "I tell you, your suggestion, long before Pearl Harbor, was a good one. That's why I began to turn to a civilian source for intelligence collecting and undercover activity. Harry, that suggestion to name our new agency: Office of Strategic Services was brilliant." Roosevelt chuckled. "Congress approved. The name sounded so harmless."

Hopkins nodded, the title did sound – so innocuous. He did not mention that some critics waggishly dubbed the new OSS: 'Oh, So, Secure,' or 'Oh, Shush, Shush,' even 'Oh, So, Silly.' He said instead, "Your move in having Donovan report directly to you was a wise one – having him staff the OSS with amateurs, not military spooks. Civilians don't get mired in traditional, bureaucratic rivalry."

The Tangier Option

"Right. And Harry, here's another example. Among various espionage sources is my friend Vincent Astor. As you know, he controls Western Union. What you may not know is that very often his people intercept foreign codes. He passes them directly to me."

Hopkins ventured, "This disaster at Pearl, it's not the fault of our people in command there." He was aware that Commander-in-Chief, U.S. Fleet, Admiral James O. Richardson had protested to Roosevelt about keeping the fleet in Hawaii. The Admiral understood the harbor's vulnerability to attack.

Roosevelt frowned, tapped cigarette ash into a silver tray. "General Short and Admiral Kimmel will have to go. Pearl Harbor must have scapegoats."

Hopkins changed the subject. "Franklin, the important thing is no one can blame you personally. Now voters will now understand why you created the OSS."

Roosevelt nodded appreciation, reached down to rub Scots Terrier Fala's curly hair. Hopkins, sensing his input into the proposed radio address no longer needed, departed coughing. He had not been well for some time.

The President' steward brought the before dinner cognac. Sipping, FDR's thoughts ranged widely. After anger came a sigh of relief on thinking that he no longer needed be a juggler; not letting his left hand know what his right was doing.

To hell with looking neutral, everything is different. At last I can openly support Britain now that we are at war with Japan. Germany soon. No more threat of impeachment by all those damn anti-war isolationists . . . that Chicago Tribune newspaper . . . that corrupt Senator

Burton K. Wheeler . . . that fascist-on-the-radio Father Coughlin. And too Senator Borah, he has got to be the most god-awful political mouthpiece for those America Firsts.

Both sets of steel braces now removed, Fala nudged his master's leg. The President acknowledged his dog's look while thinking about Donovan who had made the sacrifice, put aside his Wall Street law practice to give him full time with OSS. He will have more time for clandestine operations, for intelligence analysis.

Roosevelt swirled the amber liquid while still reflecting. Yes, everybody admires and likes Bill Donovan. Well, not quite everyone – not Cordell Hull, my own Secretary of State. He has little use for what he calls amateurs. That man still thinks his diplomats can do a better job collecting intelligence.

Hah! Diplomacy, all talk. Espionage is action. He ignores Donovan's World War One bravery that daring that earned him both a Medal of Honor and nickname 'Wild Bill'. Yes. I think I'll persuade him to leave his New York law office – Come here to the War Office, report to me – Promote him from Reserve Colonel to Brigadier. That'll give him clout in Washington. He can expand my new intelligence agency operation. Make it aggressive.

Roosevelt rubbed his withered legs. Donovan likes me to call him: 'My secret legs'.

The next day, less than twenty-four hours after the Japanese attack, Roosevelt, assisted by two aides, went to the Capitol. Ten minutes after his address to Congress, House Joint Resolution 254 declaring War on Japan passed with a final vote of 388 to 1.

Back in the oval office, the red telephone with scrambler attached rang. FDR said, "Hello Winston. Let us scramble." He pushed down the large button alongside the cradle.

Connected by transatlantic cable, Churchill wasted little time in offering condolences on Pearl. Instead, he asked for an immediate meeting in Washington with military staff to begin coordinating war strategies.

"Agreed. Arrive soon as you can before Christmas." Roosevelt put back the receiver and the scrambler automatically clicked off.

Churchill was so eager that he and twenty-seven cryptographers set out by train early on December twelfth to Gourock, Scotland to board the battleship HMS *Duke of York*. The long voyage through gales and seas was so heavy the destroyer escort turned back leaving the battleship vulnerable to U-boat and Focke-Wulf aircraft attack.

Over Christmas, numerous joint meetings between the two countries generals and admirals were blusterous, fearsome. No decisions were made on future combined actions.

Chapter Three

The President's speech in congressional session Monday had been broadcast by short wave radio.

Espionage leaders around the western world heard it themselves or received immediate transcripts. Each pondered its impact. What new initiatives would be necessary now that America was formally at war?

In London, the old Broadway building was a warren of SIS offices with wooden partitions and frosted glass windows. There early on the Director General of the British Secret service presiding over its occupants had been Sir Cummins, code-named 'C'. Now, in a more elegant suite on the fourth floor, Miss Pettigrew brought Stewart Menzies, the current DG and officially 'M', a copy of the Roosevelt speech. Sir Menzies wondered how far his MI.6 should cooperate with the President's new OSS. The American amateurs were noted for leakage of intelligence secrets. Last week he had learned a certain U.S. Lieutenant commander Butcher had left a briefcase full of documents stamped SECRET in a Washington taxicab.

In Tangier, Morocco, at his office desk in Trafalgar House, Colonel Ellis the British SIS agent and Consulate Attaché sat sipping a cup of flavorful Earl Grey tea and pondered.

While the Home Office had sent its Tangier Consul a cabled dispatch referring to America's entry into the war, London SIS had not bothered to inform him. Perhaps 'M' thought Tangier unimportant for contingency planning. Or maybe North Africa was considered lost to the puppet Vichy French regime because its Admirals fumed over their lost honor. In 1940 the British Royal Navy 'Force H' had sunk the pride of the French fleet anchored in its Mediterranean base at Mers-el-Kebir, Algeria to prevent its use by Germans.

In Casablanca, Morocco, under the crystal chandelier of the former French Ambassador's villa, German army Major General Theodore Auer clicked off the short-wave receiver.

Always wanting to appear genial and known as Teddy, he stretched his brown booted feet under the bombé mahogany desk embellished with gold ormolu and chuckled, spraining to an Oberhauptfuhrer in a side chair: "The American lamb showed teeth. Now we have real work to do."

His ham fist clenched the padded leather armrest. That fist had started his career in the mid thirties. Then, as an early enlistee in Hitler's brown-shirt storm troopers, many times he marched the streets of Berlin, arm thrust high in salute. When not marching, he smashed windows and broke the heads of *juden* shopkeepers. Ambitious, seeking promotion in a new career, he became an informer – of his comrades indiscretions or errors.

Now General Teddy Auer's intelligence cover in Morocco was an assignment to the German Armistice

Commission. This was created to insure shipment of thousands of tons of Moroccan foodstuffs and millions of tons of minerals such as iron ore, lead and phosphate to needy Vichy France. But in fact stevedores faked bills of lading and ships altered course soon as leaving port – cargoes were diverted to use in Nazi Germany. His secret role as spy, one relished and executed with zeal, was Chief of Abwehr Espionage. He reported only to the Director of Military Intelligence, Admiral Wilhelm Canaris. It would help to know which spy agency would get more espionage funding from Herr Hitler, that of Admiral Canaris or General Schellenberg.

In Paris, France, Walther Schellenberg sat in a Napoleonic chair listening to Roosevelt's speech. He wondered what America's entry into the war might do for his career in the Secret State Police.

Reichsführer Heinrich Himmler, a close confidant of Herr Hitler, had created that SS, more formally known as Geheimestraspolizei. He also tested and nurtured as protégé the young thin-faced lawyer from Saarbrucken who joined the SS at age twenty-four. By age thirty-one Himmler had made this ruthless Schellenberg a Waffen-SS Brigadefüher and Chief, Foreign Branch, Nazi Intelligence. He was always polished and elegant with silver thread forming the SS patches on the freshly pressed collars of his gray uniform. He also was resourceful, skilled and cunning.

It was in October of 1939 when he earned promotion to General as a consequence of the 'Venlo Incident'. Hitler, convinced British Intelligence was behind an attempt to assassinate him, wanted Schellenberg to kidnap and interrogate British SIS officers in Holland to find out the truth. But SS Himmler and Schellenberg had their own objectives. Wanting to sound out British reaction, they pretended to represent an underground of elites and officers who wanted a peace treaty rather than war with England. Their plan and its execution were both brilliant and dangerous. Schellenberg was about to go to the highest level in London when Hitler vetoed the action.

This momentous day that both complicated intelligence and increased its scope, the SS General's polished fingernails clicked the desktop's glossy Carrara marble. Future needs anticipated, he had planted agents in much of the western world. Yes, although General Auer had a hundred agents in Tangier, he had thought few necessary there. One SS Casablanca agent had been sufficient to send stacks of coded messages in a German diplomatic bag. These were the usual noise and chaff without substance. Now North Africa had become worthy of more attention, more SS agents.

The spymaster ordered one of his Paris most reliable and adept agents, one who spoke three languages, to report to his office.

Early the next day, Herr Goëritz, using his mother's maiden name as code, sat and heard General Schellenberg tell him of a new assignment.

"Now that the Yankees are at war with us, North Africa is of strategic importance. Go to Tangier. Be social, meet people, speak ill of Germany. I will give you further instructions at the appropriate time."

Forty years old and much too fat, Harry Richardson – his actual name – disguised his flabby body with a white jellaba as did religious Muslims. Underneath the flowing garment, trousers held pocket change and a 7.65 Mauser semi-automatic favored by the Waffen-SS. On his head was a Saudi-style headress wrapped with two black ropes originally used to hobble camels. He looked silly and harmless – ingenious cover for a spy and assassin.

Like the best of them, he was born with nerve and a capacity for self-justification. This chubby son of a British father had spent childhood in Palestine. There his father put the boy to working the digs. The archeologist searched for Judean artifacts under Roman walls in East Jerusalem and in the desert sands of Sinai. Others like Schlieman had made fame and fortune looting Maya pyramids and temples in Guatemala and Honduras. Lord Elgin wrenching marble sculpture from the Athenian Acropolis had donated them to the British Museum. His father found nothing.

The son grew accustomed to enduring long periods of discomfort. Later, educated in one of the better public schools, he was subject to bullying because of his belly. Most of the time he learned to forestall it by making up stories. He grew to hate anything Jewish or British.

After World War One, the employment situation in Germany was dire. A wheelbarrow full of German marks with six zeros overprinted on the paper money might buy a loaf of black bread, if available. The country was at a boiling point. Herr Hitler's *Mein Kampf*, written in prison, stoked the flame, established him as leader of the revitalized Germany.

Richardson read and swallowed Hitler's message. He became a survivor stealing from Jewish shopkeepers, later an informer for black-shirt fascists. He was rewarded with a transfer to SS operations and given weapons and clandestine training. He adopted a businesslike attitude and became a 'facilitator', a specialist in risk removal. After five secret and successful missions, General Schellenberg, always alert to talent with a specialty in assassination, promoted him to counterintelligence. That work he enjoyed.

He also changed names again – to Daoud.

Chapter Four

At the top floor of the San Carlos Hotel, Pensacola's most prestigious and impressive building an officer had fingers curled around a tumbler of Old Forester bourbon.

Jernigan frowned at his mirror image in the hotel bar, wishing he had this drink in Weissman's saloon. Known as Trader Jon's, the shack was a treasure trove of memorabilia hung from the ceiling – large models of Baron Richthoven's Folker triplane and U.S. army observation balloon with uniformed dummy leaning over the wicker basket's side; the walls covered with Navy squadron patches. But he couldn't go there. His classmates would still be celebrating their carrier assignments; those that is, who weren't at the Navy Chapel marrying pretty local girls.

The bartender fiddled with radio frequencies. Frank Sinatra was singing the romantic ballad *Stardust*. Jernigan slammed his right fist on the bar. Why hadn't his Change of Station papers come through? Too many days without orders.

Unlike Navy midshipmen, he had previously been commissioned second lieutenant upon graduation from the army R-O-T-C program at the University of Colorado. The war and his father in the Pacific made him change from

Army to Navy. Instead of Ensign upon graduation from flight training, his rank became Lieutenant Junior Grade.

Ready now, and waiting for him at Abbott's store on Palafox Street in Pensacola, was a brass-buttoned blue uniform whose sleeves glistened with one fat gold stripe and one thin. Now it mattered that the thin stripe had not been earned at the Naval Academy where his father had graduated. At the time he hadn't been interested. He wanted to be a geologist, study mountain rocks.

The bartender tried a different station, glanced over his shoulder and said, "There, I've got it. The President's on WCOA."

Jack put down his glass in dismay, listened in rapt silence.

"Yesterday, December 7, 1941 a day that will live infamy, the United States of America was suddenly and deliberately attacked by naval and air forces of the Empire of Japan. I ask the Congress – "

Jernigan checked the time on his government-issue watch with its phosphorescent sweep hand and olive drab strap. Not too late if he hurried.

Headquarters Building at the Pensacola Naval Air Station faced a tall white-painted ship's mast from which flapped the Stars and Stripes. He hurried into the adjutant's office, braced to attention and saluted. The Lt. Commander, a pilot familiarly known as Bird-Dog, smiled to see JJ and casually touched hand to forehead in return. In the First World War he had earned his call name Bird-Dog by an uncanny ability to spot far off enemy aircraft.

"I just heard the President speak," Jernigan said. "I've got to get into this war."

The three-striper grinned. "Take a look at this. Just came in."

Jernigan reached for the telex, quickly scanned the four lines, read it again slowly. "What does it mean?"

"It's straight forward if a bit mysterious. It's from BuPers in Washington, a travel authorization. Looks like they have an assignment for you. Sounds important."

"Great, Commander, what – "

"I've already cut Travel Orders. We've got a C-47 going to Cecil Field, Jacksonville. Maybe from there you could bum a ride to D.C. If not there's always the Flagler train going north."

A big smile creased Jernigan's tanned face. "Thanks, Commander."

"Don't waste too much time. These orders are stamped: URGENT."

Jernigan urged the light-colored Negro to drive faster. But the man persisted in driving the taxi with southern courtesy, giving all pedestrians crossing the streets the right of way. Jack had the door half open and dollars tossed before the taxi came to a complete stop.

The Navy Bureau of Personnel occupied the middle deck of the new three-story wood Munitions Building located on the Constitution Avenue side of the National Mall. Inside, Jernigan saw clerks shuffling paperwork – matching requests for ship's officers, ordinary seamen, aviation mechanics, gunnery mates for cruisers and battleships. Dozens of other needed naval ratings were being matched with appropriate personnel files and everywhere there was a sense of urgency.

With difficulty, after being told interviews were never given, Jernigan found Lieutenant Commander Stewart in his small cubicle. The officer seemed more interrogator than interviewer. After brusque questions on Jernigan's background, level of experience in flying, he asked him if he wanted sea duty.

"Doing what Sir? You know I'm not a carrier pilot."

"Admiral doesn't say. Maybe co-pilot on Dumbo, that's a Catalina PBY, or perhaps some other amphibian. You know, we also catapult scout planes from cruiser decks."

"Nice of you to give me a choice. You could have just cut orders for one or the other assignment. What is this all about, Sir? You have my file on your desk."

Commander Stewart shot him a hard look, opened and read the personnel file then reread the travel order. "Hmm, seems there's some foul up. You're not supposed to be here. Supposed to be in Norfolk, Virginia. You report to Hewitt. That's Rear Admiral Henry Kent Hewitt. Got that? Better hustle; catch a train at Grand Union Station."

At the vast naval complex occupying the Norfolk waterfront, Jernigan saw ships of the Atlantic Fleet belching coal smoke and preparing for sea duty.

After several inquiries and shrugs, he was redirected elsewhere, to Admiral Hewitt's HQ in the Nansemond Hotel in nearby Ocean View. There, in a makeshift anteroom, Lt. Commander Esperson snapped, "What took

The Tangier Option

you so long?" He didn't wait for a reply, opened the inner door.

Admiral Hewitt eyed Jernigan standing at attention, found a file amidst other documents on his desk and without wasting time on preliminaries said: "Relax, Lieutenant. Your father and I were roommates at the Academy. If you're anything like your dad, you'll measure up for this assignment. That is if you want to volunteer for something I can't explain in detail."

Jernigan hoped his confusion didn't show. "Sir, count me in."

Hewitt, a large man with salt and pepper hair took his time lighting a Havana cigar while assessing the young man. "I am leading a new Navy mission," he said, "and, I am picking my team." He looked at the glowing ember. "What security clearance do you have – Confidential, I presume?"

More mystified, Jack said, "Yes sir."

"Not enough. As of now you are cleared for 'Secret'. Even so, I can only tell you so much. Here's what I want you to do. Go to Morocco. Find a civilian aircraft and fly the Atlantic coast. Photograph, map and report any military features you see: tanks, anti-aircraft cannon, airbases, that sort of thing."

Automatically, Jernigan said, "Yessir," while thinking no combat, a photographer in some godforsaken place no one ever heard of. He also wondered why the Admiral didn't note the absence of gold wings on his chest.

As though reading his mind, Admiral Hewitt grinned and said, "A geologist with a small aircraft exploring for minerals doesn't make carrier landings.

23

Geologist – that's your cover. Report to, discuss this only with the Naval Attaché at the Tangier Morocco Consulate. That's Lieutenant Colonel William A. Eddy. Oh, one other thing," he grinned again, "you don't have enough rank for this assignment. Congratulations. As of now, you are promoted to Lieutenant. Two full stripes. Subject to congressional approval of course." He stood to shake hands. "Give my regards to your father."

Chapter Five

Pearl Harbor changed millions of American lives.

In Beverly Hills California, April Kearfoot emerged from the pool and onto the tiled patio, a towel draped over sunburned shoulders. Mother Julia, reading *Motion Picture Magazine,* looked up. "The President is about to speak. It's not just another one of his fireside chats."

April got comfortable on the tile floor, long legs dripping and folded under. She watched father Ess, his real as well as movie name, twist the large knob of a new Stromberg-Carlson 'superhetrodyne' radio in its ornate wood console. He seemed aggravated, tuning from station to station, each crackling with static.

Or maybe, she thought, he was still miffed because she decided not to relocate closer to home after her graduation in Washington. She insisted on hoping for a State Department job abroad; he believed movie making was far more rewarding.

Both parents had been movie stars in the black and white silent era. Their careers had skyrocketed after their Foreign Legion epic, *Flicker in Morocco,* premiered on Broadway. But now, twenty-eight years later, both were content to play character roles in color movies and enjoy frequent lunches at Chasens On The Boulevard.

April had grown up in Hollywood. Many times as a child, Ess had driven her in his Duesenberg convertible down Hollywood Boulevard, past the huge buildings of Warner Brothers. At Metro-Goldwyn-Mayer in Culver City, he had starred in westerns. That studio was a megalopolis with thirty-two sound stages and a main street where she had walked gawking at the outdoor sets. She became familiar with the façade of her father's western saloon – the façade propped up with wood two-by-fours. Like one large family, other actors noticed and welcomed the beautiful child; Jimmie Stewart patted her bottom.

By age ten April had no illusions about Hollywood, its make-believe. Starlets having to run around producer Zanuck's desk before gracefully ending on his couch was real. By age forteen and in Hollywood High School, she watched classmates stuff rubber falsies into tight sweaters. She didn't need them. Her graduating class had not one virgin.

Julia knew Sam Goldwyn from early times before he became a film producer and she an actress. Back then, in a Gloversville, New York sweatshop, he had been Sam Goldfisch. Both had sat long hours sewing gloves. Here in Hollywood, Goldwyn arranged for one of his producers, Benny Shulman, to meet and screen test his friend's daughter.

Although reluctant, two days before the test, April met mister Shulman for lunch in the Polo Lounge at the Beverly Hills Hotel. During luncheon she didn't feel out of place to be seated so close to Clark Gable, Ava Gardner, Jimmy Cagney and other MGM stars as they ate Columbia River salmon and Angus steaks.

Shulman, too, had been in the film business since its early days in New York. Later he carved out a niche in 'B' films. His movies, slightly better than sexploitation, usually featured wannabe starlets playing volleyball at Laguna Beach and one or another young baritone who could make teenage girls squeal.

Shulman took one look at her blond hair, pale blue eyes and revealing blouse and said straight out, "You're gonna be in my next film, in the studio water tank. It's gonna be a big water spectacular. I'll have twenty girls circling in the water and kicking legs. You dive right into the middle. Whadda you think?"

April rolled her eyes.

He leaned across the table. "Listen. You'll have to do a test because Mister Goldwyn wants new talent screened. He likes to make sure the girls are photogenic. Not that he ever uses that word but that's what he means. So when he finally says, "Okay, so put her on contract," I'll tell him I want you for my next flick: 'Beauty and Brawn'."

April's thoughts of stardom vanished when the radio speaker crackled and an announcer said: "Stay tuned for the President of the United States, Franklin Delano Roosevelt."

The family sat in stunned silence as the President recounted the magnitude of the disaster at Pearl Harbor followed by his urgent call for American effort and sacrifice.

Father Kearfoot, fists clenched, swore. Mother looked at April and thought, thank God I had a daughter, not a son.

April visualized an exciting wartime Washington. Her professor had virtually guaranteed her a job in the capital. A graduate of his Georgetown linguistics program who completed Arabic as well as the more usual French and German courses was sure to be employed.

Chapter Six

Back in Washington, April felt pleased that Professor O'Callahan had so quickly returned her call.

With urgent voice he suggested they meet without saying why. April placed the receiver back in its cradle then descended the Graylyn's three flights of creaking wooden stairs. She heard soft music escaping from under the door of the owner's suite.

Mrs. Morrison, savvy and motherly, owned the four-story townhouse converted to apartments and rooms. She also owned, next door to 1741 NW 'N' Street, the adjacent sandstone townhouse plus another directly across from it. All of them housed State Department visitors. More permanent residents like April resided on the Graylyn top floor. Her apartment looked bare with bathroom, bed, hotplate and wood wardrobe. Old District of Columbia townhouses had no closets.

April thought enjoying a cup of coffee in Mrs. Morison's ivy covered rear garden would be lovely this crisp morning, but there wasn't enough time. She nodded to Sam the Manager in the small foyer then began her walk along 'N' Street to Nineteenth Avenue, then downhill to 'M' Street where she turned west and crossed the Rock

Creek Bridge into Georgetown. She always found it exhilarating to walk this route to and from the University. Especially so when cherry blossoms were in bloom. But this morning she wasn't walking quite that far and it was too soon for blossoms.

April entered Clyde's, her favorite pub now crowded with more military than civilians. She found a small table, eased into one of the bentwood Thonet chairs, ordered a coffee and waited.

She watched a small group of WAVES, chattering and looking smart in their blue uniforms and blue brimmed white hats that sported the brass officer insignia. Maybe now that war was declared, she too should join the Navy instead of hoping for a job with the State Department.

The Professor was late. After fifteen minutes, she ordered a hamburger. Clyde's burgers were renowned in Georgetown as juicy, thick with onion in the middle and kosher pickle alongside.

April savored the last bite of pickle as the Professor arrived. In his usual corduroy trousers and tweed jacket with elbow patches he stood frowning outside where the large window glass had been swung open. He searched the smoky room for her and motioned.

April quickly joined him. Although articulate and stimulating in his linguistics seminar, Professor O'Callahan, tall with thinning hair, seemed aloof. Usually with a favorite few, he held court and relaxed with students over a beer here or at the Georgetown 1776 Restaurant. Other than grunting "Good Morning," he was introspective as April matched his stride in the two blocks to Thomas Jefferson Street, then down one block to the cobblestone landing of the Chesapeake and Ohio Canal. There, a massive timbered split gate of a wood lock controlled the water depth. Dick and Jane waited. The two mules were harnessed to a floating wood barge.

Only after the twosome was seated and Tony the barge master and hostler had the mules pulling the small barge westward did the Professor answer April's repeated question: "What's this all about?"

The youth of today are so impatient he thought, eyes twinkling as he looked across the aisle at April sprawled opposite on a narrow bench. He began to pack the bowl of his curved stem pipe with tobacco from a leather pouch.

"Sorry about all this secrecy. The necessity for it has been hammered into me so I'm doing the same with you." He struck a match and watched the tobacco begin to glow.

"Professor!"

"All right." He glanced at the barge master whose mules knew the way. "No ears here. I had a visit from an old Army friend." O'Callahan sucked in and blew out smoke. "You didn't know I served in the First World War, did you? In the Fighting Irish, the 69th New York Regiment. Well, the point is our Colonel, now Brigadier General William Donovan, didn't call me to reminisce about that war; he came looking for my recommendation. He thinks linguistic students would make suitable State Department employees."

"Yes, yes. But what does a general have to do with me? With the State Department?"

"Donovan knows our language department at Georgetown teaches French to students going into Foreign

Service at State. But he wondered had any learned Arabic. If so, he wanted my opinion."

She started to speak but he waved his pipe. "When I told him about you, he got excited."

"Why?"

O'Callahan, glanced at the barge master, leaned closer. Donovan said, "A girl! Perfect for a spy."

April, eyes large, leaned back against the barge railing. "Me? What would I . . . where would I be spying? Against whom, Germans?"

"Now you know everything I know. Donovan didn't answer any of my questions. All he said was: 'Tell her if she's interested be outside the Graylyn tomorrow morning at eight and wear a flower'. A woman is supposed to meet you, take you to an interview."

O'Callahan, after another glance confirming the muleteer was at the tiller, whispered in her ear "Don't tell anyone about this."

April breathed deeply, wet her lips. Her mind raced. She did not know what to say. Excited, her body warm and flushed, she rose and stared at the canals stonewalls, then at the clear water. "Professor, don't look," she said.

April pulled her dress over her head, tossed it on the bench then dove into the cold water. For several minutes she swam alongside the slow-moving barge, then clambered aboard. "I'm okay now." Stretching out on the bench, she said to the staring professor, "I'll dry off in the sun."

Chapter Seven

Townhouses in urban Washington D.C. have no porches or verandas. April felt silly standing in front of the Graylyn with a rose plucked from Mrs. Morison's backyard flowerbed in her hair.

She had just decided she didn't want to be a sneak, do underhand things as a spy when a black Buick Roadmaster pulled to the curb of one-way 'N' Street. A burly woman got out, grabbed April by the arm and hustled her into the back seat. She drove down hill toward Foggy Bottom and over to 2340 NE 'E' Street without a word.

This is too much hocus-pocus, glum April thought, especially so when she was ushered into a shabby old apartment building, an annex to the monumental State Department offices. Cardboard file boxes stacked along both walls made narrow its musty corridor. Nothing in the hallway suggested the occupants' functions: no plaques on the walls, no names on doors gave a hint.

Inside, General Donovan's office looked very ordinary except for two flags against the wall. Behind an ordinary desk sat a large, well-groomed man with silver hair.

The OSS Director placed a high priority on staffing his new intelligence agency with amateur talent. Usually recruiting the type he wanted at his New York offices, he was known to say: 'It is easier to train an honest citizen to engage in shady activities than to teach honesty to a person of dubious background'. Each agent personally selected had demonstrated characteristics of energy, initiative and smarts. So far, all were Princeton, Harvard or Yale graduates, most Wall Street lawyers, bankers or advertising consultants.

Temporarily in this D.C. makeshift office, he motioned candidate Kearfoot to a chair while his candid blue eyes appraised her. The Professor had said she was attractive.

What an understatement.

April sat down, stiff and taut.

General Donovan, sensing Irish charm needed, jerked a thumb backward. "Noticed you looking at my regimental flag – the New York City Fighting 69th. World War One. Old stuff. We're here to talk about this new war, aren't we?"

April had also noticed this General was in civvies, not wearing a uniform. She relaxed a little. "Yes. I mean no. I've been thinking this over and – "

"Of course you have. Now that I see you in person I've got some ideas too."

"What I mean to say is – "

"That you don't like the idea of spying, do you?"

"That's it exactly . . . Sir."

The Tangier Option

"You probably don't realize what a rare and valuable asset you can be to your country, especially since Pearl Harbor."

April didn't know spies were called assets but instinctively didn't like the word and grimaced. It sounded too impersonal, cold blooded.

Donovan quickly sized up the situation. He didn't want to lie to this young woman. Wouldn't. What's more, she would need training and he couldn't ship her off to the Camp in Ontario, Canada or that mansion in Fairfax, Virginia. Neither facility was yet operational. It would have to be Plan B with this candidate. He said, "Your Professor tells me you speak Arabic."

"Classical. I don't speak any dialects. Anyhow General, please understand – "

"Miss Kearfoot, let *me* be clear. I'm not suggesting you join an espionage outfit, get involved with covert operations . . . nasty, dirty activities. O'Callahan says you've an interest in working for the State Department, in Foreign Service. Isn't that so?" He leaned closer.

"Yes, but – "

"My sources in State next door tell me an Arabic speaking person is urgently needed abroad, in the Tangier Morocco Consulate. How would you like to be in foreign affairs in such an exotic country? Where you translate and interpret secret reports? You could make use of that Arabic you worked so hard to learn."

April's eyes shone. She would love Morocco. She loved 'Casablanca' with Bogart and Bergman. She loved reading the *Rubaiyat* in her literature class. The professor had the job description all wrong. She knew the General

35

was sugarcoating the job. But Morocco! Going to another world as a staff person in a consulate!

"General," she said, "I'd be grateful if you would arrange it for me."

That same afternoon, General Donovan introduced April to the Deputy Assistant Secretary of State for Middle East and North Africa Affairs. In a whirlwind of visits to numerous offices, he shepherded her throughout the bureaucracy. She was photographed for her passport, given the manual on 'Customs and Behavior for Personnel Serving in Foreign Countries' and signed an employment agreement that stated terms and conditions, salary and housing allowance.

In the blank space for job title he wrote: Cryptographer Assistant Officer.

She grinned. "That sounds so impressive."

Three days later, she swelled with pride during the swearing-in ceremony with six other new employees. The Assistant Secretary of State said, "Please raise your right hand and repeat after me inserting your name." April repeated after him: "I, April Kearfoot, do solemnly swear that I will support and defend the Constitution of the United States against all enemies foreign and domestic, that I will bear true faith and allegiance to the same, that I take this obligation freely and without any mental reservation or purpose of evasion, that I will well and faithfully discharge the office on which I am about to enter, so help me God."

Bursting with the good news and back at the Graylyn, April called her parents. Maybe she needed reassurance too. Of course she couldn't explain in detail what she would be doing. It was so hush-hush. Everything was happening so fast, all without explanation. Although bewildered, she fantasized about being a Hedy Lamar and having a throaty Charles Boyer on an Arabian stallion emote: "Let me take you to my Kasbah!"

Julia and Ess were supportive and had their own news. The President had appointed Daryl Zanuck to be Lieutenant Colonel in the Army and asked him to mobilize the movie industry. The MGM producer wanted both her parents to help the war effort. Julia was pleased to be acting again, even though it was a propaganda film. Her role? A mother hugged her volunteer son off to fight in his new army uniform. Ess, in turn, was assigned to a training film production unit. First assignment? A training film showed how a crusty sergeant defuses a dummy enemy bomb. He grinned, quite a switch from acting the dashing western hero.

April hung up, took a cold shower. She was too excited to relax.

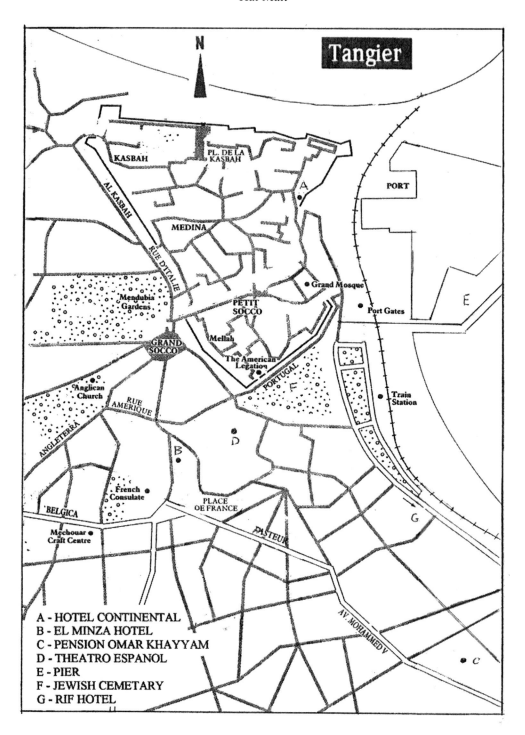

Chapter Eight

Jernigan, in the copilot seat of a twin-engine bomber was bushed and disgusted.

He had ridden buses to Newburgh, New York where, at Stewart Air Base, he hitched a ride with an Army Air Corps pilot who was ferrying the Hudson Aircraft from the Lockheed factory to England via the Great Circle Route, refueling at Gander Newfoundland, Greenland and Iceland. To top it off, the pilot alongside wore a fleece-lined bomber jacket and boots. Jernigan, in his navy uniform was freezing at altitude. Worse, the aircraft did not have dual controls. Although the one wheel, instead of joystick, could be swung over to him, this pilot refused to let him fly the aircraft and certainly not navigate.

With nothing to do, left much to his own thoughts, he brooded over his horrendous failure in the carrier crash. That failure reflected not only on him but also on his father. Even though the two not been very close, what with so many absences and navy duties, there was affection, there had been good times. His thoughts skipped to his Navy classmates on some carrier, fighting the war in the far off Pacific. He felt guilty. Here he was, trained and fit, wanting to fight too. He resolved to make good in this new assignment, no matter what it was like, whatever he had to do. In time maybe father would forget his shame.

Much later, at 21,000 feet in an unarmed four-engine British Lancaster bomber bound for Gibraltar, Jernigan began for the first time to enjoy this new adventure. Sitting jammed between sealed diplomatic pouches on a makeshift bench over bomb bay doors, he shared his peanut butter and jelly sandwiches with the Royal Air Force crew and complemented the pilot on his shiny new aircraft.

"Liked my old Lancaster better. That crate could take a lot of shrapnel, not fall apart on a rough landing."

Watching the sunrise over that huge rock jutting into the Mediterranean Sea further improved his attitude. With a new day, a new opportunity, he chafed to arrive – begin his new job.

At nightfall, in order to minimize any sighting by a lurking German submarine, the *Mayne*, a small yacht owned by a British Royal Army Major ferried him across twenty-three miles of the Strait of Gibraltar. Stacked high on board were crates of grenades and rifles and a diplomatic pouch that made Jernigan wonder what he was getting into.

At the secluded beach in Malabata, Morocco, an Arab began loading the crates onto a truck and a gray Plymouth sedan awaited him. Its grinning Moroccan driver wore a turban displaying a shiny brass U.S. Navy insignia. From the back seat Lieutenant Frank Holcomb introduced himself as assistant to Naval attaché Lieutenant Colonel William A. Eddy. Jernigan's first glance at the assistant's uniform confirmed both men held the same rank. He shook hands.

Holcomb asked him what was the date of his promotion.

Jernigan laughed and said: "Two days ago."

Startled, Holcomb looked puzzled, then smiled. "Well, I am the senior officer. What we will do now is get you checked in at the Minza Hotel. It's Tangier's best and you can get an American breakfast."

"Thanks. I'm hungry."

"It's also where Colonel Eddy has an office although our official Naval Attaché one is in the Consulate. He'll be arriving at the Minza, soon. He drives a Lincoln Zephyr. Don't be surprised if he limps. World War One wound. Shrapnel, you see."

Holcomb didn't ask what orders Jernigan had. He continued to speak about Tangier, Muslim culture and a few worthwhile places to eat.

Jernigan, watching hilly scenery and farms pass, let Frank ramble on.

"You know, most of Morocco is a French Protectorate, really a colony, governed by the Vichy government in France. But we're lucky Tangier is different. This is an International Zone – that northern point of the continent where the Atlantic and Mediterranean meet. Everybody calls Tangier the White City. And you know what?"

Jernigan, tired and hungry, lost patience, "No. Cut the tourist stuff. Tell me about Colonel Eddy. If you don't mind."

Holcomb eyed his passenger, hesitated. "Did the Admiral say why you are assigned here?"

Jernigan nodded. "He said: 'Reconnaissance'."

Holcomb grinned, "That's a nice word for it. Welcome to our city of spies. Would you believe every major country has an espionage thing going here? Some are really big operations. As for Eddy, here's the story. The Colonel is the son of missionary parents in Lebanon and Syria; after the first war he taught English at Dartmouth. General Donovan recruited him from the presidency of Hobart College this past June. That was before Pearl Harbor. Very sharp, you see. He's in charge of Intelligence Operations here in Morocco. We're modeled similar to British covert and counter intelligence MI.6."

"Never heard of it. Where does your, I mean our, Naval Attaché office fit in?"

"The office is our cover. We don't report to the Consulate headed by R. Winton Cavendish. His title is First Secretary and Interim Charge' d' Affairs. For three years he's been trying to get the State Department to name him Consul General."

"This Eddy sounds interesting. Tell me more."

"The Department appointed twelve vice-consuls for duty in the five important Moroccan cities. Eddy's the one for Tangier, also in charge of the others."

Holcomb, watching the driver swerve to avoid a donkey heavily laden with bulging sacks that were slung to both its sides, continued, "Unofficially, we call these amateur agents: 'the Twelve Apostles'."

This was getting confusing.

"What do these agents do?"

"Officially, they are designated 'Food Control Officers'. They check to insure American foodstuffs, minerals, cotton – stuff like that which is supposed to go to France – doesn't get transshipped to Germany or Italy. That gives them access to many sources of information."

"How do they communicate?"

"Each of these guys reports intelligence back to Spymaster Eddy by short wave radio wireless. Our set here in Tangier is code named MIDWAY."

Jernigan began to lose his uneasiness about this secret world, began to feel part of the team. "What kind of intelligence?"

"Maybe the Colonel should take it from there."

"Thanks, Frank."

Lieutenant Colonel Eddy understood why General Donovan had recruited him for Tangier: his military service record plus knowledge of North Africa and Arabic. Appointed Naval Attaché, he had been given control of both military and civilian agents.

All too often he felt an inner conflict between his missionary do-good childhood and the subversive role he played as spymaster in a neutral zone in wartime. It was a curious sort of existence. On the one hand he had to keep up the pretense of a diplomatic assignment. On the other hand it was his responsibility to recruit agents and get results. Achieving this goal was difficult. Unlike the British, America had no tradition, no school and no organized instruction to teach the tricks of the spy trade. Eddy felt he was running a zoo or insane asylum—the civilian inmates were a weird assortment of amateur spies, all too impulsive, too independent and not secretive enough.

This morning had started poorly. Scowling in his sparsely furnished suite on the second floor of the Minza Hotel, he hung up the transoceanic scrambled telephone.

The conversation with General Donovan had not gone as hoped. Eddy had sent him a telex memo stating: 'German Armistice Commission in Casablanca is a nest of two hundred enemy agents. Our Casablanca vice consul has provided their names, rank, duties. Permission requested to assassinate all German agents of the Abwehr General Auer. They are spies and fair game.'

Donovan hadn't liked the idea. He responded: 'War time or not, professional code prevails. Spies do not kill each other.

And now, at this moment, there were several pressing issues to deal with at the consulate. That shrew, Mrs. Cavendish was complaining again about the noise at night above her bedroom window. He knew it came from his clandestine radio, which he must now move from the roof. Unbelievable. More important, some spy was stealing decoded messages from our code room. To top it all off, the telex on his desk was from a Rear Admiral he never heard of. Seems a Lieutenant is arriving with some hair-brained mission. Eddy wondered if this officer would feel he was working for him or for his Admiral. This could be like interviewing another administrator for Hobart College, someone the Board sent him that he didn't ask for and didn't want. The Lieutenant probably didn't know didly squat about the spy business and he would wind up having to save his neck.

Just then Holcomb entered and said, "Colonel, Lieutenant John Jernigan is here." He closed the door behind him.

Lieutenant Colonel Eddy returned Jernigan's salute, said: "Welcome aboard, Lieutenant," while looking at him through spymaster eyes. He noted Jernigan to be just over six feet, broad shouldered and probably 185 pounds. He liked his demeanor, the erect posture. Probably played halfback or end in football; could do well in a tough spot. But, on the other hand, he was still irritated. He didn't need a third assistant, this protégé of a Washington admiral.

Jernigan eyed the close-cropped haircut and five rows of ribbons on the uniform of his new boss. "Thank you, Sir. I'm ready to go to work." He handed Eddy a sealed packet.

While Eddy scanned the five Photostat sheets of military career, Jernigan did a quick glance around the sparse office. On the desk was a pen and pencil set with brass plate that looked like a retirement gift. A bookcase nearby contained military manuals, books with Arabic titles, a *Tales of Chaucer* and leather-bound *Momsen's History of Rome.*

Eddy looked up. The telex from Admiral Hewitt had been brief. "What exactly did the Admiral say your mission here would be?"

"Reconnaissance sir. I am to rent an airplane and act like a prospector for minerals – cobalt, manganese and iron ore. My real mission is to scout out French military installations along the Atlantic coast. Then I send the information, maps and sketches, in sealed diplomatic pouches to Norfolk. In college," he added, "I studied geology. I know minerals and how to plot data on maps."

"The General said *you* would send back the information?"

Lieutenant Jernigan sensed he was starting this job on the wrong foot. "Sir, that was just a figure of speech, not an order."

"Hmmph! Amazing what Norfolk doesn't know. For quite some time the British have been flying camera-equipped Spitfire's from Gibraltar. Photographic maps of Moroccan and Algerian defenses are being printed in England right this minute."

Jernigan hesitated, said, "Sir, Admiral Hewitt was looking for something unusual such as Vichy French tanks or ack-ack guns. Things that might be hidden under trees."

Eddy paused, thin lips parted in a thin smile, thinking. How would a fleet admiral know there was more to intelligence than observation, looking down from an airplane? You needed to get inside the enemy's headquarters, steal plans or documents. Penetrate.

Struck with a new thought, Eddy wondered what would Jernigan's reaction be to use of his flights as cover for more dangerous espionage operations. No, this Jernigan looked like a straight arrow. He would of course agree. But better to wait a while. See how things went. Instead, Eddy said, "Lieutenant, run the admiral's mission. Fly that recon even though the British have done it. On your return you'll be working for me. Understand?"

"Sir! Understood."

"Now know this: Morocco is a neutral country and you are in an International Zone. When you run those military flights out of uniform and out of the Zone, every Günter, François and Humberto will think you a spy. You will have no protection from our navy. If your cover is blown I won't know you. The French Foreign Legion who control the Atlantic coast will make you disappear as will the Spanish Foreign Legion on the Mediterranean coast."

Jernigan thought this Colonel is one hardboiled egg. "Understood sir."

Eddy nodded. "Good man. Go to the Tangier airport. Contact the mechanic. Name is Ahmed. He will help you select and rent an airplane. But assume you will be under surveillance soon as you start flying. Remember, all actions here are observed and reported by some government's spy."

Moving on, he said, "I noted you were Army before Navy. Know the rifle and pistol?"

"Marksman, Expert and Sharpshooter badges, Sir." He watched the Colonel open the deep bottom drawer of his desk, surprised to see him lift out a .45 caliber Colt.

"1911 Regulation-issue U.S. Army side-arm. Not easy to carry or conceal, but very effective at close range."

Jernigan thought this Colonel sure doesn't sound like any college president or missionary. He took the semi-automatic, hefted the 38-ounce weapon, jammed it in his jacket pocket and asked, "How do I communicate?"

"You will meet Captain Browne from our consulate office. He will be your controller. For contact, you will need a code name. What nickname did your classmates use?"

Jernigan grinned. "Flying, my call name was: 'JJ'."

"Good enough. Don't come to my office in the consulate unless essential, then only at night. We don't use the local telephone. It's tapped. Remember to keep an eye out for surveillance. You don't have a tail now but will soon. Got all that?"

"Yes, Sir!" As he left the office, the main thing that stuck in Jernigan's mind was that he would be flying again.

Father would be proud.

Chapter Nine

April delighted in her posh, first class adventure aboard the Boeing eight-engine Pan Am Clipper. The flying boat flew to Bermuda, refueled and now was en route to Lisbon. From there, she would have to cross Spain by train to Malaga and take a ferry across the Strait of Gibraltar to the port of Tangier.

On board the Clipper, when another passenger questioned the reason for her travel, she responded as instructed: "I'm a reporter for a woman's magazine, doing an article on the effect of war on women in other countries. My readers might find Morocco exotic and intriguing." April did wonder why she, a Foreign Service employee, needed to lie. After all, she would be just a cryptographer. Maybe it had something to do with Muslim countries being male dominated.

No one was at the Tangier seaport to greet her. It was Friday, the Muslim holy day of rest and little activity. So, using her Arabic, she found a taxi driver to take her to the massive wall around the old city, the Arab medina. There, the driver pointed to the stone stairs and archway.

In the narrow, mysterious looking lane above, she was relieved to see, large and conspicuous on a building's wall, the colorful seal of the United States of America. In

Arabic, she asked the Moroccan guard at the massive wood door to see Consul Cavendish. "Come back tomorrow," he replied. It was Friday and he had no instructions to admit anyone.

Tired and frustrated, she found another small blue Fiat taxi that took her around the other side of the medina, to the Hotel Continental. Her guidebook had made it sound luxurious and cosmopolitan. But she soon found out differently. The wood planking of her second floor room was buckled and slanted. The narrow bed was a heap of lumps. Instead of a closet there was a massive wardrobe occupying much of the room. But upon opening the louvered wood shutters she saw the busy port docks and marveled at the view of the Strait of Gibraltar beyond.

The next several days were a blur. In the morning, after she bumped her two large suitcases down the stairs to the small lobby, a military looking man in plain clothes greeted her. He introduced himself as U.S. Army Captain Gordon G. Browne, Assistant Naval attaché. He didn't need to add he was her boss. The way he looked her over, April wondered if he had expected an old hag.

The Captain told her she could either get a special rate here if she liked the hotel or he could take her to a pension, one with a private shower and toilet. Hoping to control at least the choice of her own home, she said, "I'd like to see other places, choose later and stay at the hotel for now."

"No problem," he said. April soon learned that in Tangier everyone said: 'No problem.' No matter big or small the issue, or whether they would do anything about it.

The concierge was nowhere to be seen. Browne put her luggage behind the desk and said: "First, I'm going to take you to the consulate." He impressed her as no nonsense all business type. She could handle that.

Driving the gray Plymouth down the narrow winding alley lined with small shops, Browne began her briefing, telling her he was happy to be relieved of coding and decoding responsibilities. He refrained from saying 'chores.'

Browne abruptly braked to miss hitting an Arab whipping a tiny donkey then said, "From now on, you should not be seen with me. It will arouse suspicions, blow your cover." April was confused, didn't know she had or needed one. "This town," Browne added, "is loaded with enemy spies."

In the consulate, while she hurried up and down stairs, through courtyards trying to keep up with his long strides, Browne recounted the history of the complex. It had been an ornate palace presented by Sultan Moulay Sulieman to President James Monroe in 1821.

"The real story," he said, "is it was no gift. It was reparations for so many Barbary Pirate attacks on our sailing ships."

All that sounded interesting and not in the guidebook. But April wanted to talk about her job, about who sends classified messages and what equipment there was.

Browne replied that scrambled messages could be sent or received by radio, telex or cable. "Our short-wave transmitter uses a separate code. Maybe later you'll get to do decoding from that one too."

He wouldn't tell her its location. Annoyed, April wanted to say she was supposed to be a cryptographer, not merely a code clerk. Instead, stopping in front of a tinkling mosaic tile fountain in a courtyard, she asked: "The consulate sounds like a busy place. Why so much secrecy?"

"Okay. Here's the local situation. Tangier is an International Zone – a stew pot full of French, Spanish, Italian, German spies."

"Germans?"

"Here they are based in the Rif Hotel. Over one hundred of them occupy an entire floor. The other spies are located in their countries' consulates. And they unlike us have more than one intelligence agency." He paused – "Let's put this in context. Because of rivalry between their separate but equal agencies, none of them share information. The Russian military intelligence at home and abroad, the GRU, fights with its civilian rival, the larger KGB. The British SOE who do sabotage and the SIS who are cold fish and a bunch of bastards, don't talk to each other. The Germans have both an SS and an Army Abwehr competing for Hitler's approval. Here in Tangier, I am a State Department vice-consul but don't report to Mister R. That's R. Winton Cavendish. He is Chargé d'Affaires, an Interim Consul in this State Department Building. Instead, I report to Colonel Eddy who is not only a vice-consul but also Station Chief for the OSS. Confused?"

April thought that was some mouthful. She asked, "To whom does Colonel Eddy report?"

"Save that for later." Browne hesitated . . . "We in Intelligence don't talk about our activities with anyone else. Not even someone on our own side."

On arrival in the basement code room, Browne introduced her to Joseph Cyran, the army signal corps clerk code-named STORK. April could not help noticing on the workbench, the open *Esquire* foldout of a buxom Petty Girl.

"Sergeant," he said, "We have a new member on our team so you can stop bugging me about some help. Meet April Kearfoot."

Cyran grunted, "Glad to meetcha," while appraising this good looking doll. He had expected another signal corps enlisted man.

"Give her all the German and French intercepts."

"What about my Arabic?"

"Arabs don't use codes. It's rare to find one that can even write. But I have an idea we can talk about. Later. After you settle in."

Leaving, he said to April, "You will be in good hands."

Sergeant Cyran's pride in his work soon overcame reservations about a woman sharing his office and job; welcomed her to the Snake Pit. Garrulous, he began to show and describe the various equipments and functions. Then he mentioned that the Germans and British have very complicated code machines but our State Department uses a simple code based on the paperback *Webster's New Edition Dictionary*.

"The way it works," he said, "is like this. Using six figures, the first three numbers represent the page. The fourth figure can mean anything from one to nine. Odd numbers mean column one, even numbers mean column two. The last two numbers tell you the number of words down the column from the top. Browne frequently changes the page."

April felt a tingle of anticipation. "Let's get to work."

She knew she was not mathematical. She was a linguist, one who always found language fun. She also enjoyed a challenge. But coding she soon discovered, was tedious. Moreover she was supposed to be an analyst, not just a clerk. Browne had said the consulate now had sixty-five employees. Sergeant Cyran complained the number and frequency of messages had more than doubled since Pearl Harbor.

Later that afternoon, after his own break, he glanced at April. She had been analyzing and cramming the stream of decoded messages into file folders for hours without a lunch break. One blond curl had fallen over her forehead and her pencil pointed motionless at a page. He said, "Let's get some air."

With coffee cup in hand, he led up a series of disconnected stairways to a large flat roof. "We can talk here," he said. "Our code room is probably bugged. Browne says there's a spy in the consulate."

He ignored April's questioning look and gestured toward a small wood structure. "That shack is where we used to have our short wave radio but missus Cavendish, she complained the tapping noise of the Morse key was keeping her awake at night. You have to tap forever, you know. So we moved our equipment . . . it's in a suitcase and has an aerial strung down a drainpipe at Eddy's villa. He rents the villa from Mister Sinclair."

"Is Sinclair important? Who is he?"

"Sinclair is the retired Governor-General of Zanzibar. But that meant we had to have MSG's twenty-four hours. Too expensive."

"MSG's?"

"Marine Security Guards. So we moved back to that other shack across the alleyway."

"Who works the radio?"

"My corporal. He sends and checks for coded short-wave radiograms. Of course he doesn't understand any of it. Didn't Browne brief you on all this?"

"All he said was there were many codes. Why so many?"

"Keeping it simple, I have . . . he glanced at her and chuckled. "*We* have to know these different codes. For example. Mister Cavendish uses his special code to send all those memos to Washington asking permission for this or that or explaining why he has problems with the French or Spanish ambassadors or how come he has a spy in his own building. Cavendish is very nervous about the State Department, you know. He's not an Ambassador, not Consul not even a regular Charge of Affairs here. So State hasn't a clue on our North Africa situation."

"Does Colonel Eddy?"

"You betcha. He gets coded reports from that bunch of amateur vice-consuls: lawyers, stockbrokers and such. There is even an anthra, uh, anthro-pol-ogist. That one has a pair of calipers; runs around a mountain measuring the head of some tribesman or other."

Eager to know more, April questioned the sergeant about the vice-consuls, their duties, especially spying.

55

"I don't know much about that," he said, "neither does Cavendish and we don't tell him. You know, their spy reports, all that stuff, it's no good. I'll just say, they think their shit is better than anyone else's.. I've handled most of their transmissions. Maybe you'll get to help me."

"I hope so. But you keep long hours."

"So here's the scoop on their transmitters. Our Tangier transmitter is code named MIDWAY. The Casablanca one is LINCOLN run by AJAX. Algiers is YANKEE, run by a Frenchman named Frederick Brown. PILGRIM is Oran. Also in Algeria is FRANKLIN. They all have different codes. We have to learn each so if one gets busted, the whole network don't shut down." He tossed his coffee dregs over the side. "Let's get back to work."

After several days April found the work dull and routine. She rarely encountered a message to be analyzed that sparked her curiosity. Soon she worked mechanically, until one day she realized something was wrong. It continued to bother her. She checked the file drawer, then checked again. The British SIS folder *was* out of sequence. It had yesterday's decoding where the Naval Attaché office was asked to mobilize small boats and carry foodstuffs to Malta under siege. Could someone be stealing our secrets? What was going on. A cold shiver went up her body.

When she told him, Sgt. Cyran laughed. "Impossible," he said. "Only employees with security clearances can enter this room. Every night I secure that file cabinet. See that flat steel bar over there in the corner? I jam it down behind the drawer handles of the file. It goes into this socket at the base. See? Then I lock it at the top." He hefted the huge padlock in his large palm.

Chapter Ten

The airport 17 kilometers south of Tangier appeared desolate. It boasted one paved and potholed runway, a small terminal building and one tin-roofed aircraft hanger. On the tarmac adjacent to the structure seven ragged looking airplanes were tied down with frayed ropes.

Inside the hanger, Jernigan saw an Arab clad in greasy green coveralls kneeling and bobbing on a small prayer rug facing Mecca.

After learning the Arab's name was Ahmed, Jernigan jerked his thumb at an aluminum airplane with three huge radial engines at the far end of the field. Its corrugated dark green fuselage, showing black stripes and a white swastika on the rudder could not be a Ford tri-motor.

"Junker. Ju-52," said the mechanic. "Teddy Auer's. Flies it to Vichy France."

"And who is the blond guy staring at us?"

"Van den Goosen. Dutchman pilot. Also supposed to be flight engineer, but knows nothing about engines."

"Where did you learn such good English?"

"English man in villa Old Mountain. I service cars, Drop-head Riley, Rolls-Royce."

As they walked along the line of tail draggers on the rutted tarmac, all squatting nose high over their close spread front wheels, Jernigan explained he was looking to rent one. Suddenly excited, he zeroed in on an antique French biplane – a Nieuport model 17 fighter. He knew it from his readings of World War One allied aircraft. Its silver painted fabric looked shabby and the red, white and blue stripes on the rudder faded. No Lewis machine gun was mounted atop the upper wing, but it had its 9-cylinder rotary engine. The 110 horsepower Le Rhone looked OK.

Ahmed, with a sly look said, "This one no good for you. Too small. You go to Spain. Buy old Lebel rifles and cartridges. Maybe 7.2 Mausers? Sell them to Berbers, to General Tassels in Rif Mountains. Fight French. Yes?"

Jernigan thought this man talked too much. This had gone far enough. He pulled out his wallet, showed his official-looking commercial pilot license issued and stamped by the U.S. Department of Commerce and said: "I explore for minerals, for cobalt, iron ore, phosphate. You Understand? I will test fly this airplane."

Ahmed stood aside.

In the single seat Jernigan buckled up, checked joystick and rudder pedal movements. The instrument panel had holes where gauges had been removed. The two remaining ones looked odd. No matter, probably didn't work anyhow. You flew this crate by the seat of your pants.

Jernigan flipped on the magnetos, yelled "Clear."

Ahmed put both hands on one of the propeller's two laminated wood blades, spun it. On the third try the engine coughed, sputtered then smoothed into a reassuring ticking. The biplane slowly rolled ahead. With forward

The Tangier Option

vision blocked by the engine cowling, Jernigan fishtailed the plane from tarmac to grass and after glancing at the fluttering windsock, pressed a rudder pedal to turn into the wind. After all, this fighter was built for the green fields of France, not asphalt. Left hand on the throttle, he 'poured on the coal'. The tail came up and in seconds he was airborne and happy as a clam: *I'm flying a fighter.*

No matter the fighter was from a previous war. The wires stabilizing the wings hummed just like the PT-17, the 'Yellow Peril' he soloed in primary training. At 1,500 feet he leveled off and breathing rapidly, once again became a hot pilot doing every remembered aerobatic: loop, split-S, Cuban eight, barrel roll and eight point slow roll. He was in heaven.

Satisfied, he cruised in lazy circles over Tangier, noting the thick stonewalls of the medina, admiring the sunny vista of white buildings that straggled up the seven tall hills.

According to the glass vial hung from the top wing, almost all fuel was gone. Time to land. Jernigan aimed the plane at the tallest mosque minaret and, engine screaming, dove down to rooftop level and flew around the minaret. After, on a straight-in approach to the airport, he buzzed the field at twenty-five feet, zoomed up in a steep climbing turn, came around and landed near a cluster of men that included Colonel Eddy and Captain Browne. As he climbed out, a tall Arab in a white robe and skullcap went ballistic waving his arms. He ranted, raved, pointed skyward.

Eddy, grimfaced, explained. "You buzzed this sheik's mosque, largest in the city. Its minaret points to Allah. You violated his airspace."

Taking Jernigan by the arm, Browne hustled him away. "You are not supposed to know," he said. "That sheik is our valued agent. Code named 'Mister Strings'." Browne did not add that the sheik, God's representative to the radical Islamic Brotherhood, had been bribed with fifty thousand dollars. That was how he built his tall minaret.

Jernigan laughed. "Nobody will think *I'm* an asset after that public exhibition."

No one meeting the tall, blond South African at the airport would take him for a Nazi agent. He was far to open faced, affable and handsome, perhaps too much so.

It was two weeks since General Auer's pilot disappeared and the General appointed Van den Goosen his replacement. Although a Wehrmacht army position, it was normal for the Gestapo to become aware of any appointment of a non-German. It was *not* normal for SS General Walther Schellenberg to be aware of such low level decisions.

However, his deputy suggested: "This Goosen's army assignment to the Tangier Junker presents us with a covert opportunity to have our SS plant inside the army's secret service. Beyond his task of ferrying the Chief of the Moroccan Abwehr across borders, he could be a double agent who reports not only to the army but also carries out espionage assignments for our SS. Could be perfect."

So Goosen had been 'invited' to meet a high SS official and now, sitting erect and cautious, listened as

General Schellenberg leafed through the green bound dossier and commented: "Very impressive . . . flew an airplane at age seventeen . . . navigated trackless South Africa bushveldt at night by the stars . . . was recruited by Abwehr in Holland. Successful in your last three army espionage assignments, you are self-reliant." Schellenberg looked up. "Unfortunate about your father. Killed by a British guardsman in the Boer War, was he?"

"General, it happened *after* that war. In one of Lord Kitchener's concentration camps."

The SS General's nod was sympathetic. There would be no question about this man's loyalty to Germany. He closed the file, said "Ja, your father would have liked to see you in this new posting, one where you will have greater opportunity for revenge. Of Course Major General Auer, your superior in the Wehrmacht Abwehr, would not. It is best for you that he does not know you now work for the SS."

Chapter Eleven

After several weeks in the code room April was delighted when Browne invited her to the Attaché office in the basement nearby for a coffee break. Preliminaries aside, he questioned how she liked coding.

"Boring," she replied. I dream in Morse, soon I'll have to knit in Morse." Browne surprised her by laughing.

He changed the subject to an account of *his* many duties. One, she discovered was to build files on unusual events, gather information on individuals who might be helpful or harmful to the war effort. His problem was how to get to know these people, their attitudes and beliefs.

Then out of the blue he popped a question: "How would you like to help me? Great opportunity to meet interesting people, go places with a newspaper ID card."

April stared. "You mean be a spook, spy on people?"

"Not as a case officer. I call it reporting. You see, our consul Cavendish, thinks I work for the OSS Propaganda Branch. That's my cover. It can be yours too. I can arrange a part-time job for you as columnist with the British *Tangier Gazette*. Expense account of course. This rag is very prestigious, established here in 1883 and publishes in three languages. Could be Arabic too. You can handle that?"

April glowed. "Of course." She didn't mention that in French, Gazette meant 'gossip'.

"You could brief me on what's happening, who is doing what . . . work the cabarets; gather information for Cavendish's consulate bulletin as well as the Gazette. I even have a code name for you. How do you like . . . 'Hot Cat'?"

April adored the idea of a new challenge, and her name was a hoot. What a lark. She would be just like her Hollywood mother, an actress in a Moroccan thriller.

In the mornings April worked like a drone with Sgt. Cyran. In the afternoons, she enjoyed being the Gazette columnist, gathering news and gossip. She talked with dignitaries, shopkeepers, hotel concierges, bartenders and their customers. She was invited to events at consulates and art galleries. The cover allowed her to explore Tangier, its neighborhoods and souks, enjoy the sea breeze that came up the hills cooling the warm summer days. She loved it all: meeting fakirs, gunrunners, weird or pompous people in their bizarre costumes.

But when eagerly grabbing and thumbing the Gazette off the press, she found her column disappointing.

Tangier Gazette
Monday, June 8, 1942

First page headline: 'United Nations Day', pictures of Roosevelt and Churchill. In Spanish, '1000 bombs fell on Bremen during 75 minutes'.

Page 2: Picture of Fifth Avenue with the caption: '15,000 women of the Women's volunteer and defense corps marching in New York'. They wore uniforms with skirts.

Page 4: *Tanger al Dia* by April Kearfoot: Cinema Rex is showing dubbed in Spanish MGM's '*La Indomita*' with William Powell, Jean Harlow and Franchot Tone. A new lending library has opened at the British Trafalgar House. Attending Princess Alexandra's weekly bridge club were . . .

She was crushed. The editor had chopped up her submission, made deletions, made it trivial in comparison to world events.

Weekly, April turned in the column to the paper's office at Rue du Statut. Often, she tipped Browne about suspicious characters or doings. When she complained that men thought she and her column were frivolous, Browne was delighted with her cover.

"You're my best asset," he said.

If that's spying, she thought, there's nothing wrong with it at all.

Late one afternoon April told sergeant STORK she still worried about the folder labeled British SIS. Again the folder was out of place in the file drawer. Was she going daffy?

"Jeez." The sergeant took it personally. "Me myself locked up last night. For Chrissake, forget it."

Yes, she told herself going out the door, best to forget about the office. Go out tonight and socialize. Meet some interesting men; perhaps hear a little gossip for the Gazette that might be useful to Browne.

Maybe I'll go to Porte's. She's rumored to be the Comtesse de Porte, former mistress of French Prime minister Paul Renaud. Her place is supposed to be neutral territory for all nationals. As the sergeant told me: "Go to Tingis Café for food, but it's Madame Porte for tea or booze, 5 to 7 p.m."

Back in Washington April had thrown a black dress into her suitcase wondering if she would ever wear it. Now she zipped it up and smoothed it over her round breasts and hips. Looking in the cracked wall mirror, she smiled and thought, not bad for an old lady of twenty-three. Ah, she mused, but a lonely one. For the first time since her arrival she felt a pang of regret, thinking of Georgetown and being surrounded by eligible, young men.

The taxi driver knew Madame Porte's location. "Very respectable for women," he assured her in Arabic.

He sped to the intersection of two major streets, stopped abruptly, pointed and smiled. "All spies go there."

The Salon de Thé did look promising with its classical French exterior and stunning art nouveau interior that hushed when she paused inside the entrance. April gave a fleeting smile sensing so many men looking her over. She knew they were thinking – new meat in town. She would have instant success with so many to pick and choose from.

None of the men wore the Arab jellaba; most wore business suits; a few were in black, gray or khaki uniforms. In the quick scan she noticed at the bar an attractive tall blond who looked cosmopolitan and a dark handsome American. Both were worth pursuing.

Blowsy owner Porte sat behind the cash drawer, observing all with knowing eyes. April knew better than to invite companionship by sitting alone at a table. At the bar, she squeezed in between the handsome American and a small Frenchman smelling of rose water whose mustache had waxed points.

She wondered if the taxi driver had it right. Was everyone here a spy? They all looked so harmless.

The American glanced, turned and stared at her wavy blond hair, oval face with its upturned nose. He didn't waste an instant. "The name is Jack," he said, "and I'm having a Gilbey dry martini. No bourbon here. What'll you have?"

"I'll have a Manhattan," looking at the barman, she added, "and give me the bill."

While the impassive Spaniard mixed their drinks she quickly studied the American: black hair, cleft chin, lean and fit. Not a businessman, not with that raw scar showing on his forehead. No man cuts himself shaving there. She wondered what besides the weather would make a safe subject? Then she decided to let him make a move.

On cue he said, "I've only been in town a short time, don't know much about what goes on. How about you? And your name is?"

After telling him and that she was a reporter for the Gazette, he kept the conversation flowing. He gulped his drink; she sipped hers. He questioned her about the town, the local hot spots, what things to see – assuming she had all the answers.

April in turn was thrilled to talk with another American, this geologist and pilot looking for minerals. She promised she would write a Gazette article about him. The headline would be: 'American Explorer Looks for Minerals'.

Alarmed, he grunted "Please don't. It'll tip off my competition."

The evening slipped into nightfall. He leaned close, placed his hand on hers and she wondered what he would do next; uncertain what her response would be. At that moment, Lieutenant Holcomb, tracking Jernigan, arrived at Madame Porte's and blinked twice. There he was, romancing a blond – April! And from the look things, he was meeting with success. He hurried toward the bar. Noticing him approach, April blushed, removed her hand. Holcomb made a pretense of not knowing her. Jernigan introduced his new acquaintance, a reporter for the local newspaper.

April, sensing the situation required her to do something, excused herself and headed for the toilette. Holcomb grabbed Jernigan's arm and whispered: "Eddy wants to see you. Now."

When April returned the others had gone. She felt foolish. Looks like I've been dumped, she thought.

Leaving the bar, the incident from this morning about the misplaced file flashed into mind. I'm still bothered. Not sure why but I've got to go back to the code room.

At his Minza suite this morning, Eddy was crisp and to the point with his two assistants. "Washington finally made a decision. Now we get cracking. Jernigan, your orders are to get on the ball with the Admiral's aerial coastal survey; be sure it's accurate. I've asked General Donovan to send you ASAP a reconnaissance aircraft. Meanwhile get your butt to the airport; make do with whatever's available. Holcomb, get him enough money from funds in the Attaché safe." When Eddy was under stress he sounded more like a Marine martinet than a former English professor.

At the Consulate, the Moroccan guard opened the massive door. Holcomb took Jernigan into and through the labyrinth of patched together buildings down to the Naval office in the basement. Four times he twirled the tumbler of the old gray safe painted *Marvin Safe Co.,* twisted the small knob handle and took out a large bundle of French francs. "These francs are the equivalent of three thousand in U.S. dollars," he said with a grin, "Don't spend it all in one place. And you will need this.

He pulled out a file folder labeled: Gov Info Maps. "Shows part of the Atlantic coast."

Jernigan unfolded the stiff paper, read the title: *Great Britain, War Office and General Staff. G.5 4241.* "Not what I need," he said. "Look. It's a military grid, doesn't show roads or towns. It's an artillery map."

April's feet hurt.

She took off the stylish leather pumps she had chosen to color coordinate with her dress. The cool tile floor felt good as she padded down the corridor to the code room. A splinter of light shone beneath the door. Had she left a light on? April eased the door open an inch.

A single bulb in a small reflector illuminated the file drawer with its long steel bar now pulled out and, at her desk, a stout figure clad in a soiled dress bent over a Minox camera mounted on a fifteen inch tripod. The Spanish charwoman, *Photographing decoded messages!*

April plunged headlong into the office. She grabbed the stout woman by the waist – wrestled, struggled to lift her off balance, knock her down. The muscular woman's work-hardened hands grabbed April by the throat, squeezed.

Locked together the two staggered around the room. April broke free. The woman punched her in the stomach. April couldn't breathe. Leaning away, her hand reached out, groped for the letter opener used to break seals on the dispatch bag. The woman charged head first at April. The letter opener's outthrust point tore open the fleshy neck; pierced the charwoman's artery. The woman screamed once.

Blood spurted in an arcing geyser.

"Did you hear that?" Jack looked up from the Michelin map he found on a bookshelf.

Holcomb shrugged. "Damn tom cats again, always fighting."

Chapter Twelve

Over the Atlantic Ocean
June17, 1942

Prime Minister Winston Churchill struggled to be optimistic.

At midnight, during his hastily arranged travel in a Boeing flying boat, his thoughts turned again to the American president.

So far, my dealings with Roosevelt have gone better than expected. Maybe, because each of us face public criticisms—our loss of Singapore and so many British colonies, this week's humiliating news that Tobruk in North Africa has fallen, the desperate feeling that England is near death. With Roosevelt—it's his lack of action after Pearl Harbor. Yes, we two leaders share mutual problems with critics at home. This morning when I called saying: "It is urgent we have another person-to-person consultation," Roosevelt knew it too.

Of course it was. Those naïve Americans – hardheaded Army Chief of Staff, General George Catlin Marshall and Navy Admiral Ernest King – both insisting on invading Vichy France. My Commander in Chief General Brooke knew it would be a bloody disaster.

Too bad I had to prove it by ordering trained commandos to invade the Norwegian coast. So the Germans massacred two thirds of that force – our sacrifice made no impression on the Americans! What an appalling lack of understanding -- Forty-seven German divisions across the English Channel would be facing those unprepared, untested Yanks . . . suicide.

Somehow, instead, I've got to convince FDR to invade North Africa. He must relieve our British troops retreating back across the desert to Alexandria. That's less than two hundred miles to Cairo. An allied invasion would squeeze that 'Desert Fox' Rommel, get him in a pincer between American troops to the west and we British to the east.

Weary, Churchill shifted restlessly in his leather seat and stared through the porthole unseeing at the sea below. If that isn't reason enough, dictator Stalin, that two-face, is pressing us for an immediate second front. I would too. Hitler has got half his army at Stalingrad. He's making it a smoking ruin. So Stalin continues to yell if Russia fell, those same troops could cross the Channel to England. Yes the situation is iffy. Roosevelt must understand that.

Churchill walked forward, sat in the co-pilot seat for half an hour enjoying the sensation of soaring amidst the stars. Soon he retired to the 'Bridal Suite,' so named because a double bed occupied most of the cubicle. He opened the official pouch handed at departure by his private secretary, pawed aside decoded telegrams and documents to find her daily letter forwarded from 10 Downing Street.

The familiar salutation: 'My Darling One' and her personal news, as always, gave him release. This time Clementine wrote of sending all the servants away for a week's holiday except the tall housemaid Lena who with Smokey the cat were looking after her. She expressed concern that son Randolph had left his regiment to join a parachute detachment of the Special Air Service. And she felt certain this trip should prove more fruitful in results than his visit with that ogre Stalin in his den.

"Amen to that one," Winston said aloud. The letter fell from his hand, he fell asleep.

After flying twenty-seven hours, passing over Gander without refueling, Captain Kelley Rogers prepared for landing the flying boat on the Potomac River. The Prime Minister, again in the co-pilot seat, nervously pointed ahead to the Washington Monument at 550 feet tall. Rogers smiled and touched water before hitting the obelisk or two bridges.

In the White House, Harry Hopkins had arranged the meeting agenda. Two critical operations, each Top Secret, required an immediate decision. On arrival, Churchill was hustled into the Oval Office where greetings were cordial if brief. Before Churchill had time to light a fresh cigar, Roosevelt posed the first subject – code name: TUBE ALLOY. Hopkins, sitting tensely, listened as the two strong personalities debated this first issue – atomic energy.

British Intel, it seems, had discovered German scientists working at the Norse Hydro Company in Rjukan, Norway. The Nazis were building a heavy water and centrifuge plant. Churchill, moreover, spoke glowingly of his British scientists' progress in nuclear fission at the Clarendon Laboratory in Oxford. He continued to press for control of all allied nuclear efforts: "Already we have discovered how to bombard uranium to form barium and krypton gas. We are ahead of both the German and your own efforts and are planning a bomb making factory for production in Canada."

Hopkins watched the President bristle, become adamant. Underneath that jovial exterior, he could be hard as nails. FDR said forcefully: "The atom bomb must be an American effort for use against Japan!"

A strained silence followed until, with a wave of his huge cigar, Churchill acquiesced. His primary concern concentrated more on the second operation, the unrealistic one proposed by General Marshall and Admiral King. Unfortunately, Roosevelt supported their plan to invade Vichy France – code name BOLERO. It was exasperating.

From the disastrous commando experience in Dieppe, France, Churchill and General Brooke both knew that any effort to invade Europe would require a minimum of one hundred fifty thousand troops. No doubt these Americans would be raw recruits and neither the U.S. nor Britain had the ships to transport that many. What made it worse was that the Yanks had that peculiar American 'Can-do Attitude'.

Hopkins had to admire the way Churchill hammered his main point—the North Africa situation looked bleak. The British 8th Army needed relief from General Rommel's Panzer tanks. General Montgomery could not hold on much longer before being pushed out of

North Africa. England also had to consider a possible cross-channel invasion to its shores from Hitler's one hundred fifty thousand troops in Vichy France. England was desperate. Vulnerable.

Of course, FDR knew all this. He had his own pressures. Almost daily, Stalin was pushing him hard for relief of Stalingrad. The angry Russian leader would shout that America must open up a second front. He kept repeating, one to the south of France would pull fifty or more German divisions away from their brutal siege of his Stalingrad.

Churchill wasn't budging.

He once again carefully proposed the British staff plan code-named: GYMNAST, a more modest proposal for a military invasion of thirty thousand troops into North Africa.

"This," he said leaning forward and tapping his cigar ash, "will satisfy Joseph Stalin."

For his part, FDR responded with typical pride that America already supported Stalin. CEO Wilson at General Motors in Detroit was making Sherman Tanks, shipping them to the Russian port of Murmansk. And CEO Larry Bell's Niagara Falls, New York factory was cranking out Bell Aircobra P-39's by the hundreds. Most were flown to Fairbanks, Alaska then across the Aleutian Islands to Russia.

Hopkins sighed. FDR's was no solution, not nearly enough. He had advised the President that a troop build-up meant a delay. It would be impossible to invade Europe before the November elections. For political reasons, action before then was urgently needed, the sooner the better.

Roosevelt, stubborn, insisted still on an all out effort across the Channel.

The fruitless meeting between two bull-headed leaders adjourned without decision.

In spring and summer, to escape Washington's sticky heat, FDR frequently spent weekends at the family home in Hyde Park, New York. Two days after their White House meeting, he met Churchill at the local airport with tilted cigarette holder clamped between teeth and driving a black Packard 160 convertible, top folded down.

"Get in," he said to Churchill. "I'll show you the scenic route." The chubby Prime Minister saw the car had no pedals, no clutch.

Roosevelt drove off in fits and jerks using levers on the steering column. At the edge of the Hudson River escarpment, Churchill took one look down the precipice, grabbed the door's frame, closed his eyes and held on.

Together after dinner, with port wine and cognac, the two Allied leaders relaxed. Roosevelt put another cigarette in his long ivory and ebony holder and Churchill's Partagas Corona smoldered at half-length. Roosevelt pursed his lips, watched his curl of smoke rise then glanced at his guest.

"Winston, I have reconsidered my position . . . primarily because I know we have thirty thousand troops ready and eager for action. Even though I have just dispatched a fleet to help protect Australia and Asia I can still put together a limited convoy of ships and aircraft. So this is what I have decided. I will order General Marshall and Admiral King to cancel all planning, for Europe. For that BOLERO effort I was pushing. Instead we will go to North Africa with you."

Churchill beamed, said: "Franklin, a wise decision. I will advise General Brooke to meet with your Chiefs. Put together a Plan."

"Good. I suggest you go into the Mediterranean, somewhere east. We will land on the Morocco Atlantic Coast also push east. With your General Montgomery on the west, General Brooke will have Rommel in his pincers. I suggest a code name for the invasion: TORCH."

Churchill, smiling inwardly, readily agreed then immediately worried about American laxity of security. "Franklin," he said, "you know as well as I there will be horrible consequences, a major disaster if there is the slightest leak as to date and landing place."

Roosevelt raised his glass in a toast. "To a military gamble. Morocco in October."

Chapter Thirteen

Jernigan arrived at the airport dressed for his explorer's role. To look the part he was wearing his old khakis and knee-high mountain-climbing boots.

For this lengthy flight, he had resolved to spend more time in selecting a much different airplane. That French fighter the other day had been a blast but impractical. No room for even a clean shirt or thermos of coffee. Last night in his pension, the French Michelin road map spread open on his mattress, he planned this cross-country flight, much as he had at the Naval Air Station, the only difference being in kilometers not statute or nautical miles.

He drew a circle around all airfields shown along the Atlantic coast, decided to fly south as far as Casablanca. Maybe there really is an American Rick's nightclub, he mused. What the hell, might as well have some fun . . . all work and no play makes Jack a dull boy.

After walking the tarmac back and forth, he paused at a high-wing four-seat Dassault. Yes, this one is roomy; it could even carry one or two heavy sacks of rock samples.

He strolled into the hanger, ready to make

arrangements. The blond pilot was there with an older man, a General. They were sitting heads together at the greasy desk that was littered with aircraft tools and parts.

Jernigan introduced himself. In turn, pilot Goosen responded by introducing himself and Lt. General Luis Orgaz, Commander Spanish Forces in Morocco and, after the fall of France, now Administrator of the Tangier Free Zone. The General acknowledged the introduction, said Señor Goosen was helping out until a mechanic arrived.

The General's cold stare chilled Jernigan's curiosity. He became all business, saying he wanted to rent the Dassault. The General slowly got up and walked out for a quick look at the decrepit aircraft, then came back to him, eyebrows raised.

"Why?"

Jernigan wanted to say, "None of your damn business," but the man was a Lieutenant General and layered with medals. He replied with a smile, "I work for a company that explores for cobalt and iron ore, maybe other minerals. In the Atlas Mountains where there are no roads."

General Orgaz did not believe this for one minute. The iron ore was in the Rif Mountains not the Atlas. And prospectors use burros in mountains not aircraft. He stood in front of the open hanger and watched the American walk toward the Dassault. He was accustomed to making quick judgments about men – his enemies, his subordinates, his peers. It had kept him alive through too many years of intrigue, suspicion and envy in Franco's fascist Spanish court.

He had a sudden thought. Yes, he liked what he saw: confidence, determination and a military bearing yet little deference to much superior rank. Such a man was a risk taker. Orgaz decided to have him watched. Perhaps when the time was ripe he could partner him with Paco.

Orgaz had always resented the 1912 Treaty of Fes. He felt it a serous mistake, an insult. It was the Spanish admirals and conquistadors in galleons who had sailed south on the Atlantic to Asilah, to Larashe, or crossed the Strait to conquer Northern Morocco, Ceuta, Mellila – all those towns colonized by Spanish long before the French arrived.

Often he brooded over the treaty King Alfonso signed that confined the Protectorate to a narrow area when the whole country should have been Spanish. He had nothing but contempt for his timid King; contempt for the Morocco puppet, Sultan Mohammad Five; contempt for all pompous French diplomats and Generals – each and every one of them arrogant and stupid. Not one, except perhaps General de Gaulle, knew how to win a war. General Franco knew enough to rely on his generals. Our army had crushed the communist Spanish Republic and restored the Monarchy. German airplanes and tanks had helped, of course.

He, Luis Orgaz, would win back Morocco for the honor of Spain. His grasp of significant events would prevail. Now this new war was truly a world war. Germany had partnered with Spain before. Would again. He would help German troops swing down from Vichy France through Spain and into Morocco – oust the French and return Morocco to Spain.

The General pondered. How could this young American, obviously a soldier, help me?

Jack felt happy as a bug in a rug. A long white scarf, bought in the bazaar, was twice wrapped around his neck, its tail flapping in the breeze. Feeling like World War One ace Eddie Rickenbacker, he pushed the heavy goggles higher up his forehead. On that first flight in the French fighter he had been so excited he just climbed in, strapped her to his ass and took-off. This morning he was going to be more careful.

On the walk-around he inspected the aileron and empennage hinges . . . rusty; tires and wheels dirty but okay; engine compartment bolts . . . okay; petrol fluid in gauge . . . okay. He buckled himself into the left front seat. The Colt semiautomatic Eddy gave him bulged his jacket's right pocket, the other pocket held an apple.

It was ten past nine before he reached 1000 feet in a cloudless blue sky. Going south, the morning air was smooth, the engine sang its song when . . . what's that? The *Baedeker Guidebook* had mentioned Phoenician tomb excavations in the coastal cliff. He dropped to 250 feet.

No soldiers manned the battery of anti-aircraft cannon that pointed out to sea; their wheels sunk into the shallow tomb cavities, but . . . a submarine just beyond! Painted on the black conning tower were white Nazi stripes. Two sailors waved him away and when he swooped lower and circled, a machine gun appeared and sailors mounted it to a railing.

Bastards. What to do? The only thing he could think of was to throw the apple. It splattered on the hull. The

Nazis laughed. Jernigan wondered: a German submarine in French waters? What kind of war is this?

Twenty minutes later he caught a glint of steel under a cluster of trees bordering a farmer's field. He landed, taxied toward the trees and, with the engine idling, climbed out of the cockpit.

A worried looking young soldier held a rifle aimed at him. *"Non, Non, Monsieur.* You cannot land your airplane here."

"Why not?"

"French army place. You see those cannon? 75-mm. No one must know they are here."

Jernigan gave the soldier a nod of understanding while taking the compact Leica from his shirt pocket. When he had questioned Eddy about the camera, Eddy had shrugged, barked something about a German spy who wouldn't need it anymore. Now, before the surprised soldier could protest, Jack snapped three exposures of the artillery installation, tossed the soldier a military salute. In another minute his engine ticking became a roar.

According to the map the small fishing village ahead was Asilah. The inlet looked small and without a beach. Not an idyllic location for military use.

Twelve minutes and twenty-five kilometers further he checked the fuel. Down to the black one-quarter line on the gauge. Time to refuel. Ahead, he spotted the somewhat larger port of Larache and inland a level clearing with an airplane alongside a shack.

Hearing the noise, a short man in a black pilot's jacket came out and with a sullen expression watched this old plane with French markings taxi toward his four orange painted steel drums. The Spaniard's expression improved on learning that the pilot with a friendly grin was an American. Not for one minute did he believe that cockamamie story about a geologist exploring for minerals. Never mind, thought the black marketer and gunrunner, the tall American probably didn't believe his story about operating an airplane charter service either. With a cheerful grin he helped the stranger pump fuel from one of his drums.

In the air again, Jack thought this trip along the Atlantic was surely a wasted effort. That Spanish pilot had said the better coast was the Mediterranean with its many airfields. And the Rif have iron ore, he had added with a sly smile.

Forty-five minutes and hundred-ten kilometers later he came to a sizeable town. Was this Kenitra? In the US, he grumbled, the town name is painted on a water tower or barn. But his mood changed on seeing a huge vista that spread beyond a wide, wriggly river to Port Lyautey, a military airbase . . . and with an all-weather concrete runway.

Circling, he counted on the tarmac maybe a hundred sixty sleek looking aircraft. Probably Dewoitine D.520s, the best French fighter against Nazis. Oh Boy. Look at those American planes: two Douglas A-20 attack bombers and six Curtiss 75-A Hawk fighters with colorful yellow and red markings on cowling and empenage. So many aircraft could give our navy pilots plenty action.

Jernigan reduced speed further, photographed the numerous airbase installations. At the river's mouth there appeared to be several kilometers of wide sand beach without rocks. According to the Michelin that beach was Mehdia Plage and the village, Fedala. He noted: 'perfect location for any invasion.'

Thinking he might be missing something, he flew inland. The snow-capped peaks of the Middle Atlas Mountains to the east were magnificent but he saw nothing unusual about their eastern slopes. He flew over the village Michelin labeled: Sidi ben Slimane. Noting a vast flat plain with no obstructions, he thought the location an ideal one for a major airbase.

Thirty kilometers further, the town of Salé appeared. He identified it by the streets sloping down to the wide river labeled Bou Reg. A large airport was located near the river's north bank and east of the town.

Jernigan inserted a fresh roll of film in the Leica and snapped several frames. He also jotted a note: 'very defensible.' Across the river on a high cliff soared the massive Kasbah walls of the capital city Rabat. Protruding through the fortress embrasures were huge muzzles of siege cannon.

And in Rabat itself the 2,500 feet airstrip alongside what appeared to be a Sultan's palace was obviously too small for military use unless – maybe paratrooper drops? He made another note.

The Michelin depicted ninety-seven kilometers to Casablanca. That would stretch the fuel, something taught never to do. He should have landed and refueled back at Salé and now the sun shone low on his upper left wing. But Rick's in Casa beckoned. He flew on.

The enormity, the activity of Casablanca's port surprised him. He gaped at the enormous size of a battleship flying the tricolor flag. It was moored in the outer harbor, away from freighters in the inner harbor. "Got to be the *Jean Bart*," he mumbled and looked at the turret guns. Must be fifteen inch, big as anything at Norfolk. And take a look at those shore batteries in bunkers. Murderous field of fire; they control the harbor approaches, suicide for our guys in assault boats.

Time to quit fooling around. Do something about fuel. The map denoted a commercial airport by the symbol of a black T-shape in a yellow square. At some distance, to the southwest of Casa, he located the large commercial airport. But he could also see, not shown on the map, a grass military airfield. It was smaller and nearer the shore. Flying over its tarmac, he got a good look at six Curtis Hawk airplanes directly beneath him. These were the P-36's he had heard about – fabric wings but the first American fighter to have an all-metal fuselage. From what he had read, Glenn Curtiss hadn't been able to sell them to U.S. General Hap Arnold.

Jack refueled at the Casa Airport but his jaunt to Casa was a bust. Rick's Bar turned out to be a seedy café full of Germans in uniform. And just like in the movie, someone was uniformed as Claude Raines playing the French colonel. No beautiful Bergman here. No use dallying.

In the Dassault he buckled seat belt and headed back to Tangier.

TNG airport had no runway lights. Late, with the engine throwing thick Castrol on the windscreen, he landed in darkness on an expanse of grass instead of the paved narrow airstrip and taxied to the tarmac. Strange.

Ahmed, who slept in the hanger, didn't come to place chocks under the wheels and do a tie-down.

Inside the hanger, illuminated by a desk lamp low wattage bulb, Jernigan stumbled on a rolled up rug. Ahmed's bloody body was inside.

Next morning when Jernigan came to the Minza office, Colonel Eddy listened to the report of Ahmed's murder but did not comment. He had already crossed out Ahmed's code name from the little black book kept locked in his top drawer. He put Jernigan's marked-up map, notes and Leica 35mm film in a white Consulate bag and sealed it. "You did not get anything further south . . . to Dakar. Why not?"

Jernigan wanted to say there was nothing to see south of Casa until the airport at Safi and what's more Dakar is more than a thousand miles further on. He said instead: "Sir, the Dassault's engine was throwing oil."

Old soldier Eddy knew he was being had. With a steely glare he retorted, "The reconnaissance aircraft General Donovan is shipping will arrive Tangier Port in three days. Use it. And no more excuses."

Before leaving, Jack reported sighting the Nazi submarine surfaced at the Phoenician tombs and asked for a bomb. He was certain he could dive bomb that sub, blow it out of the water before the crew could mount its machine gun.

Colonel Eddy sighed. "Lieutenant, we know that U-boat. Attacks British supply convoys going to Gibraltar or Malta. When its captain is under the lee of that cliff he is in neutral waters; not international. Leave it for the British to deal with. What is more, don't try to be a one-man army."

Jernigan saluted and left, thinking all the while he was ready for a drink or getting laid. He stifled a laugh. There was always a cadet rumor that their food was spiked with saltpeter to chill down randy ones from local girls. And if you weren't yet horny then you needed to buy Spanish Fly – guaranteed to make a stone statue have an erection. Yep, Moroccan women although swathed in headscarves and kaftans head to foot were starting to look good.

Chapter Fourteen

In Washington it was ten p.m. when General Donovan roused Lieutenant Colonel Eddy in Tangier on his MIDWAY scrambled radiotelephone and told him: "Be prepared for a major allied invasion of Morocco. Will inform Torch target date and place later."

Very soon, this unusual and important intelligence was decoded by agencies in other western world capitals. Foreign military and political strategists began to analyze its significance, its potential impact on their military efforts.

In London, Heads of both the British Secret Service and the British Special Operations Executive were informed of TORCH. Each leader resisted sharing with underlings this knowledge of an invasion. Suspicions of one or more moles had surfaced.

Also in London, Charles de Gaulle, leader of the Free French in exile was *not* informed of TORCH. The British considered that arrogant, self-proclaimed General had no need to know. Unreliable.

In Moscow, Josef Stalin, on receiving radiotelephone calls from both the American President and British Prime Minister became angered to hear TORCH meant North Africa. He knew from Churchill's adamant insistence that an invasion across the English Channel was impractical. That being so, he had argued strongly that an allied invasion be made through Spain into France. But no, undoubtedly those English Generals were more interested in their pincer movement to trap General Rommel in Egypt. He also fumed about the October date, so late. By then forty-seven army divisions could be sitting in what was left of Stalingrad drinking German beer!

In Wiesbaden, Admiral Wilhelm Canaris, Chief of Abwehr, the Army military intelligence service, telephoned General Keitel in Berlin to request a meeting with der Führer. He knew Hitler would want from General Keitel a detailed briefing with suggestions on North Africa – should he consider a preemptory army strike through Spain to Morocco? Also, what *is* the exact date and place of this invasion? Because General Teddy Auer in Morocco might have more current information from his spies, the Admiral ordered him to stand by for the Hitler meeting. His more than two hundred agents on permanent German payroll status might come into play. He could not know General Auer's airplane had a pilot who doubled as an agent for SS General Walther Schellenberg.

In Paris, General Schellenberg rushed to Berlin for a meeting with SS Obergrupenführer Reinhard Heydrich, widely known as 'The Hangman'.

"Eisenhower? Never heard of him," was the blond Obergrupenführer's first reaction. "He is some renegade German, I suppose."

"*Nein, mein Herr.* He was a Colonel in Texas, never led so much as a platoon in combat. Now the Colonel is a Major General leading the invasion."

"Hah! We will slaughter him."

"No doubt. But read these." He showed his boss a sheaf of intercepted transoceanic conversations. Included were comments on invasion plans by Churchill, General Mark Clark and Eisenhower's aide, a Navy Lieutenant Commander.

General Heydrich's eyes widened, indeed the news was important. He would alert Reichsfüher Heinrich Himmler at his Prinz Albrechstrasse HQ. Himmler must be the one to tell Hitler about these events threatening General Rommel in North Africa. Such meeting would be difficult. Volatile and unpredictable, Hitler had earlier announced he couldn't be expected to divine the plans of Germany's enemies, who were such 'military idiots'. However, the news was so major, so important that the SS must get it to Hitler before the Abwehr did, even if Hitler flew into one of his murderous rages.

In Paris, French Admiral François Darlan, High Commissioner of North and West Africa remained a chameleon interested mainly in prestige and pension. The advisor reported nothing of this startling and major event to the Vichy French President, Maréchal Henri Pétain. That French hero of World War One was now a German puppet in Paris, confined to his office in the Hotel des Ambassadeurs. Yes, there had been feelers to Darlan from the Americans as to French resistance if America attacked, but he liked being a fence sitter. He would weigh the significance of an invasion against his own status and career in the Nazi-controlled French regime. So he need not discuss any of this with the doddering old President.

However, Maréchal Henri Pétain in his isolated office did receive word of the planned invasion. The eighty-three year old stooge for the Germans immediately ordered all French forces in North Africa to resist whatever, whenever and wherever.

In Rabat, Morocco, Vichy Resident General Charles Noguès took seriously the rumor that Americans would invade but could not believe an invasion would occur before spring 1943 at the earliest. "Before that can happen," he told his regular army and navy officers, "there might be another raid on Dakar to the far south. No problem." A small group of army junior officers engaged in sabotage on Vichy French fortifications were elated and further encouraged.

In Tangier, R. Winton Cavendish, in a foul mood, closed their bedroom door and descended the winding, narrow staircase to his second floor consulate office. He would have to talk to Naval Attaché Eddy. While reading the *Tangier Gazette*, his wife had seen Miss Kearfoot's photograph alongside the gossip column. Puzzled, certain she had seen the woman in the building, Mary Ann asked, "Doesn't she work for you?" He had to make up some excuse.

Fact was, Cavendish realized, his fiefdom was spiraling out of control. He certified all budgets and expenses of consulate employees. Worrisome. Especially because he personally recorded in longhand all expenses in the big ledger, even those claiming 'miscellaneous' of which he knew nothing. Many of those sixty-five employees were vice-consuls or Naval office people, *employees who didn't report to him.*

Now Washington was suddenly interested in Morocco. Cables were flying back and forth. Incoming diplomatic bags were full of questions he couldn't answer. To top it off, the French consul had spoken of an allied invasion rumor and *he* couldn't even get a clear answer from Washington. Cavendish sighed – here he was, a fifty-four year old nearing the end of a three-year tour. Unlike his Foreign Service peers, his title remained the same: Interim Chargé d'Affaires, not Consul.

Chapter Fifteen

Looking at the Minza façade from the street, the uninformed would have no idea what lay beyond that plain wall's arched and embellished doorway.

Inside was a former Pasha's palace. Unlike the United States whose White House remained the residence of all elected leaders, in Morocco a change of Sultans or tribal leaders meant another new palace for each of the five Imperial Cities.

Leaving Eddy's Minza office, Jernigan descended stairs each tiled in multi-colored mosaic to an immense courtyard open to the sky. Surrounding at upper levels were numerous rooms, formerly those of the Pasha's harem. Crossing the marble floored patio, he headed for the bar, but suddenly paused.

What was it Holcomb had said during that first guided tour into town? Something about Tangier having more than five hundred bars and brothels.

Like a kid in a candy store he debated which other bar he should sample. Choices. They ranged in atmosphere from the lowbrow Deans Bar – a hangout for gays, hash smokers, prostitutes male as well as female – to the highbrow Rif Hotel. There, he had heard, the same vices were practiced but with greater finesse.

He wanted some action. He looked first in Madame Porte's. That gorgeous blond with the warm smile was not there. He strode downhill to the *Plage,* the beach location for numerous clubs and hotels along the boulevard Callé d'Espagne. Holcomb had said the Rif Hotel was the favorite hangout for German spies. Might as well have a look.

The Rif lobby wasn't much. While going up the staircase and hearing piano jazz, he looked through the landing's window and saw outside a superb view of the sandy beach. The kneeling camel on it, he supposed, was a postcard prop for tourists. Although with the war few were coming.

At the second floor, fish lazily swam in a long glass case whose top served as a bar. Sure enough, many uniformed Germans, Vichy French, Italians and a sprinkling of what might be Spanish spies crowded the bar. This Saturday night all the women at tables appeared elegantly dressed with much gold and jewels draped on cleavage. He zeroed in on April who was sitting at a crowded table. Jernigan grabbed a nearby chair and squeezed it adjacent to hers, causing scowls, reshuffling of other spaces.

He grinned at April's welcoming smile, nodded to Van den Goosen, the airman with the Junker at the airport. April rattled off an introduction to the others, starting with General Teddy Auer whose uniform bore two stars on its epaulets. The General merely lifted a thick eyebrow. Then expatriate Lady Strathmere, a brittle-looking older woman, eyed him like she might a stud horse at her country estate north of London. Jack, not knowing Lady Strathmere was a fascist aristocrat of Lady Astor's 'Clivenden Set', said hello with a smile.

"And I am Harry, Harry Daoud." That got Jack's attention – a fat Englishman with an Arabic name wearing a long, white jellaba. Harry sipped tea with mint leaves, said nothing more.

"What are you having," Jack asked April, eying her half empty glass alongside a pad and pencil. The Rif did not impress him as the place for a decent martini made with English gin.

"The local plonk. Don't try it."

"Trolling productive for news tonight?" To the waiter he ordered Spanish brandy.

April replied with a side glance at Lady Strathmere, "There's always some gossip here for my column."

"And what, Mister Jernigan, do you do?" Lady Strathmere inquired, leaning forward so he could look down her low cut dress.

Goosen smirked. "He says he's an explorer. Also a hot pilot."

"Ah, so you are the one who rattled the windows of my villa, you rascal. A celebrity for your column, my dear April. An explorer *is* a rarity around here." Her eyes sparkled.

General Auer's fingertips brushed his mustache, wider than Hitler's but just as black. "I believe you found what you looked for? During your flight south." He smiled, eyes hard as black pebbles.

The General knew. Now Jack wondered what, if anything, he would do about it.

The group of German officers at the bar began singing a beer stube song, keeping time by clinking their white steins with pewter lids. It became impossible to converse. When the Germans stood and shouted the lyrics to the Horst Wessel song, Jack leaned close to April's ear, noticed her large blue earring matched her blue eyes, and said "Let's get out of here."

They took a lengthy stroll along the boulevard, hand in hand, enjoying the seashore that looked silver under a three-quarter moon. Near the port, April's glance met and held his. Words unnecessary, she led the way climbing steep, unlit and twisting alleyways to the Continental Hotel. Twice he hesitated, looked back behind him to see if they were being followed, saw only shadows.

They sat in wicker chairs on the hotel terrace. From its famous overlook they watched the harbor panorama of pier, docks, freighters, fishing boats and the bay beyond. The view from on high, the silence and absence of other guests heightened a sense of togetherness. He looked past her golden hair to time the flashes from the tall lighthouse on the Malabata promontory. Its beacon reminded him of the one at the Pensacola Naval Air station. He tried to relax.

April thought this attractive man was different. There was something private about him that intrigued her. She wanted to seduce him but would not use the tactics honed so successfully in Hollywood and Georgetown. At least not right away.

Now watching a large freighter enter the harbor, he put his hand over hers. Damn, she was attractive. "About that geology . . . I was a navy brat. As a kid I lived in several towns. Went to four different schools . . . my father was frequently away on sea duty. I got used to living alone with my mother; treasured the bushel basket of the seashells he sent home. My father got promoted to skipper of a destroyer and was at sea when the Japs hit Pearl. He always demanded excellence of me, said I should join the Navy too . . . so I took a university degree in geology."

He turned to look at April while adding with a laugh, "Rocks are far from the sea. But the University of Colorado had a ROTC program, so here I am."

April thought all that must have made him self-reliant. Soon she had him laughing with funny stories about the family life and friends of her Hollywood childhood – the movie stars. Then she asked about his exploration flight . . . was it successful?

He shifted position in the wicker seat. Rather than answer he related his first flying experience, the one that put the flying bug in his ear. He told how his uncle had bought him a ten-dollar half-hour flight with a barnstorming pilot in a Jenny, a two-seat World War One biplane.

Then abruptly, he asked: "You must know a lot about that bunch I saw you with at the Rif. What do *they* do?"

April swung her chair around, studied him. "They all like to gossip, talk to me, because each of those bastards knows my paper would never print the hard truth. You must know by now that almost everyone you see at the Rif or Madame Porte is a spy. There's more plotting going on here in Tangier than in the Hollywood movies."

"Which, as you said, is La La Land. Fiction."

"Fiction based on reality. Let's think of Tangier as the silver screen showing a good western, like director John Ford's Stagecoach. These characters here – German, Italian, Spanish – represent vicious Indian tribes . . . Apache, Sioux, Cheyenne, all experienced warriors. Show no pain, show no mercy, live to hunt and kill intruders."

"And we're the good guys?"

"Sure. Cowboys leading a wagon train full of innocents into danger, unfamiliar territory and terrain, rivers to cross, a pass to find in the mountains. You and your grizzled sidekick, Eddy – "

"He's not my friend."

"And sooner or later you know you are going to be ambushed."

He countered, "Doesn't the cavalry come to the rescue?"

"In Hollywood it always does." At that moment she recalled three transmissions she had decoded that day. "Maybe here too, maybe your buddies will."

"Well, I'm no John Wayne. Just a geologist."

She winked. "Tangier is the place to find out who you really are."

His sidelong glance caught the change in look of her eyes. Jack pulled her out of her chair and kissed her.

April took his hand, led him upstairs to her warm bed in the small room.

The Tangier Option

Chapter Sixteen

Among the many onlookers, John Joseph Jernigan was most impatient.

The fully loaded 8,000-ton Patrick Henry, flying the Stars and Stripes, squatted low in the water yet loomed large beside two rust-streaked coastal steamers all roped alongside one of the Tangier concrete piers. Amongst the first 350 Liberty Ships built in less than a year at the San Francisco shipyards of Henry J. Kaiser, the freighter and her American four-stack destroyer escort now flying the British flag, were curiosities.

"Yes indeed." The freighter's captain answered Jernigan's query when ashore for lunch at the adjacent Royal Yacht Club. "I've had your four crates aboard since Galveston, Texas. Dunno what's inside. Sealed and stamped DIPLOMATIC they are. Should be on the dock by now."

Colonel Eddy glanced at his Navy pilot, said: "Its our reconnaissance aircraft. Our Army's nickname is 'Sentinel'. He didn't add that General Donavan had pulled many strings to have Army release an aircraft to a Consulate.

The destroyer's Captain, lighting his pipe's bowl of tobacco, looked over the flame at Colonel Eddy. "Why

101

didn't you chaps take care of that periscope I saw off shore. 'Twas less than twenty miles from here. Gave my boyos a bit of excitement, don't you know. I believe our depth charges sunk it. Saw a rather large oil slick."

By the time lunch ended, Eddy had arranged to transport the four crates to the airport. Jack would ride with crates in a lorry on loan from the British Consulate. As for the freighter's escort, the destroyer's Captain said "We're gung-ho for Gibraltar, deliver twelve aircraft. Spitfires." With a grin, he added, "I hope to eliminate more submarines."

Arriving at the Tangier Airport, Jack saw the new attendant filling the Junker's petrol tanks and motioned to him. When finished, he helped open the crates and spread aircraft parts on the hanger floor.

Curious to see what was going on, the Dutchman came from the Junker to the hanger too. He was in time to see two wing-halves come out of one wood crate, the fuselage out another and the engine and fixed landing gear cradled in a third. Out of the large fourth crate came the empennage known as 'tail feathers', a two-blade aluminum propeller, a Technical Manual titled 'L-5 Liaison Aircraft' Assembly and miscellaneous fittings.

Goosen said "I know a few things about airplanes, even small ones. Of course I will help too."

Jack hesitated. He didn't feel good about the Nazi offer, but responded to a fellow airman: "Let's assemble the empennage to the fuselage first, then the landing gear."

Working as a team, and with more tools from the Junker, the three men rapidly assembled several components to the fuselage. Its two sides, painted olive drab, featured a white U.S. star. Inside, the instrument panel displayed an oval brass plaque reading: 'Manufactured by Stinson Aircraft Company'.

All too soon it was nightfall and the attendant wanted to leave. Goosen, seemingly not tired in the slightest, announced: "It is alright. I will continue."

Grinning, Jack said "Good man." He positioned and held one half-wing with its two steel tabs in alignment with the airframe eyelets while Goosen inserted the two bolts and used his wrench to tighten them. They repeated the half wing procedure on the other side. Afterward Goosen walked to the terminal where he could get a croissant and glass of mint tea. As for Jack, he wanted to sleep in the cockpit but decided to return to the city and dream of flying his new spotter airplane.

For three days, early and eager, he arrived at the hanger in the borrowed Plymouth and with the attendant, completed installing the remaining L-5 components. As an after thought, he scoured the hanger for paint. All he could find was a muddy brown color. "Have to make do," he muttered and painted over the white stars on the fuselage and wings.

Although impatient to test-fly his new aircraft, he began a thorough preflight inspection. Slowly he walked around the high winged tail dragger, checking again the fuel connections, touching engine connections, each airfoil hinge, the rigging maze of cables and every control. Suddenly he sucked in his breath. What's with this wing? Jiggles. *The two bolts loose!*

Jack leaned against the fuselage, picturing what could happen. The half-wing, bolts not tightened, would not immediately have come apart. Instead the aerodynamics would change. After takeoff, at low airspeed, that wing would begin to flutter and flap wildly. At a hundred feet the unstable airplane would be impossible to control. In the wreckage his body would be a mass of pulp. Everybody would think him a rotten pilot.

The Junker had gone and with it Goosen. Was the man careless or worse?

After tightening the two bolts Jack buckled up in the cockpit, pushed the starter button to crank the engine and taxied off the tarmac. Airborne and climbing to fifteen hundred feet he checked stall speed. The L-5 with its very large wing flaps was maneuverable at speeds low as 50 mph before stalling. He flew three touch-and-go landings over the next half hour and was delighted. This plane could land in a very short field. That might save his life.

Driving back to the city, he decided to take April for a joy ride on Sunday. Thinking about the possibilities gave him an erection. He recalled receiving a graduation gift of a Model A Ford from his father. It had a stick shift, not the floor pedals of the original Model T. He drove that coupe west on the old Lincoln Highway to Denver then on to Boulder and the university. There, what fun it had been to take a date, clutching him in fright, around those mountain curves without guardrails. Afterward, the sex when parked on one of the overgrown mining roads was intense – even though the stick got in the way. Yes, he would show April this new airplane. Too bad he couldn't rearrange the seating.

Chapter Seventeen

The White House
Saturday, July 25, 1942

President Roosevelt struggled, cigarette dangling in left hand, to become more comfortable in his high-backed leather chair. He was in the Oval Office enduring Washington's stifling heat, impatiently awaiting a call on his scrambled transoceanic telephone.

Not so long ago he had believed his biggest problems lay with his make-work projects: WPA and all those other acronyms to which Republican senators objected and newspapers ridiculed. War had silenced most of those critics. Now his concern lay with the North Africa invasion. He knew it was a colossal gamble. This largest Armada in history, six hundred fifty ships – could also be the naval disaster largest of all time.

Prime Minister Churchill and he were fond of their countries navies. Churchill who had been First Lord of the Admiralty had signed more than a thousand dispatches to Roosevelt with code name: FNP, Former Naval Person. When Roosevelt, a former Secretary of the Navy became President of the United States he changed his code name to POTUS.

He was emptying the holder of its cigarette stub when the London call came through. He made his voice sound upbeat.

"What luck, Harry?"

The ongoing London Conference had been wrangling without success to resolve many conflicts between British and American military leaders. Worse, the strife and confusion between the American top brass itself was intolerable. No Wonder. The Coordination Manual by the Joint Board of the Army and Navy dated from 1927. Amazing. The upshot had been Major General Patton in Washington and Rear Admiral Hewitt in Norfolk hadn't talked to each other. Disgusting! Harry Hopkins at the conference was his last and best hope.

"Mr. President, our big-wigs are celebrating. All is decided. Torch will be the only joint operation for 1942. Eisenhower will command our effort even though Ike still remains skeptical. Just as you wanted, our fleet handles the Atlantic, the British fleet goes into the Mediterranean. So, Generals Marshall and Brooke have stopped butting heads. It's over. You have won agreement on all your 'must have' points."

"What about Winston, is he satisfied?"

"Yes, Franklin. Churchill agreed. Though our Ambassador Kennedy worried that German troops might come by air from Sicily or that Franco would bring Spain into the war on the Axis side to get the spoils of French North Africa. That's possible, how likely we don't know. I will confirm the conference results at length but here are the Operation Torch highlights. The original D-Day in October had to be moved to November seven. That's the last day when a winter landing on those shores can be risked."

"Acceptable. You and I know if we left the decision to Admiral King a landing would not happen until next year."

"This Plan has three parts. We are the first part called Western Task Force. That's all American. Rear Admiral Hewitt lands Patton with thirty-five thousand troops. He takes Casablanca and Port Lyautey. Second part has Royal Navy Rear Admiral Troubridge commanding the Central Task force. Thirty-five thousand British capture Oran harbor in Algeria. Third part Eastern Task Force will also embark from UK under Rear Admiral Burroughs. His twenty-seven thousand troops take Algiers. That is the gist of it, Mr. President."

"Hurrah!"

Host Hopkins went back to the celebratory party that was in full swing in his sumptuous suite at Claridges.

Roosevelt was putting a fresh cigarette in the holder when another scrambled call came through – Winston.

His call expressing a different concern was more urgent than the previous. He requested much more aid of everything. The Kriegsmarine of Gros Admiral Karl Dönitz in the Mediterranean had just sunk two thirds of the British merchant ships on relief convoy to Malta.

The important decisions of the London Conference were almost immediately known by the major Axis intelligence agencies. Their need to learn the exact date and place of the invasion became even more pressured. As for the Allies Counter-Intelligence agencies, they were ordered to prevent such discoveries at all cost.

In Washington, General Donovan, his speech rapid and voice crackling with unusual tension, spoke with Lieutenant Colonel Eddy via the Tangier MIDWAY radio saying "TORCH is a 'GO'. All top political and military leaders are on board. This is a big deal. Now you are amongst one hundred twenty five persons informed of exact landing place and date. So expect trouble from that Tangier nest of enemy assets. Count on spies given highest priority to get specifics of our Morocco Operation. I suggest you create some sort of Deception Plot."

In response to Eddy's once-again query, Donovan replied, "Colonel, I authorize all-out counter-intelligence operations. Yes, your gloves are off, International Zone or no. Where necessary, if called for, eliminate any Axis spy."

That afternoon, after receiving Colonel Eddy's orders to intensify counter-intelligence, Captain Browne entered the consulate code room. Telling the sergeant to take a hike for ten minutes, he took the chair opposite April. She put down her yellow No.2 pencil and looked at him quizzically.

"The information, the feedback you are getting as a reporter is helpful," he began. "Eddy appreciates it."

"That's nice to hear. But I've been wondering. As for my cypheranalysis, I better mention something. The most recent German intercepts don't make sense. I mean they've changed their codes. Is that usual?"

"What's happening April, is the war is coming to us here in Morocco. "

"That's no surprise, after reading so many dispatches."

"I can't give you any particulars because I don't know more myself. What I do know is you can be even more helpful."

April stared. "Doing what?"

"Run a string of agents."

Her first thought was he just took the fun out of newspaper reporting.

As though reading her mind, he added, "This is important. We need to know more, a lot more, especially how the French army would react to an invasion. You see, with your contacts, you are able to get us useful information."

"I don't see how."

"Get others involved. But keep it simple. What you should do is find one reliable person who would recruit another and so on. Soon you would have a chain of assets. Nobody else on the chain should know of you or any other. That way if one person's cover is blown, the whole thing doesn't . . . collapse. I must tell you this will be dangerous work. And you never received any training for it. What do you say?"

With a mixture of curiosity, patriotism and grit, she responded: "I can do it."

First, April tried to recruit the one person who knew everybody and everything in Tangier.

"*Cherie*," Madame Porte laughed, "you are the fourth spy who asked the same thing. Do not worry; I will not speak of this to anyone."

Next, April decided to try recruiting agents while delivering the Consulate Bulletin printed in Arabic. Full of optimism, she put several copies in a woven straw basket, dressed herself like a Berber woman and, with a hijab under her straw hat that covered blond curls, strolled into the Berber marketplace. Alongside the walled medina were rows of mountain women squatting and selling their produce on mats placed beside the narrow road. She hoped she could pass for a Berber because these women had light skin and eyes, not the darker Arab color.

To one after another she handed out a free Bulletin. Knowing the women couldn't read, she smiled and told them whatever story was printed on the front. Then she would say something uncomplimentary about Germans. If a woman nodded agreement, she made a connection between the Nazi's and Vichy French. After a week of this and putting a few franc notes in the Bulletins, she noticed the Berber women breaking into toothless laughs when taking the money. She couldn't figure out why.

The only nibble she had was Ambrose, a back packer from Brown University. The Berber women often gave him an egg, one of their fruits, or a pinch of hashish. His jeans were filthy, cowboy boots scuffed, chambray shirt soiled. No matter. He was outgoing and they liked his guitar playing.

One day he drew her aside and said: "If you want to communicate with these women you had to do so in Berber, not Arabic. They don't understand a word you say."

He added that if she wanted to communicate with any educated Arabs, she should speak in French, not

Arabic. He also confided that a German had offered to put him on the payroll as an agent, to sabotage any American invasion.

April was quick to suggest he accept the German offer, become a double agent.

Ambrose, afraid to go back to the States because he had a low draft number, thought the proposition ridiculous.

"Stuff it," he said, picked up his pack and continued moving on.

The next Saturday, April, sitting on the terrace of the Continental Hotel and drinking mint tea, thought hard what to try next. In a quandary, discarding unsuitable ideas, she suddenly pictured the lane in front of the consulate that was called Street of America. It led to the gate of the Jewish cemetery. "Jews," she said aloud: "Jews! Jews hate Germans."

April walked uphill to the Jewish Cemetery, rattled the metal gate. Standing outside in the lane, she explained to the caretaker that she worked for the American Consulate and hated the Germans and Vichy French who are murdering Jews in Europe.

"I tell you this," she said to the man wearing his Sabbath day clothes, "because we have such evil Nazis here in Tangier. You Jewish people could help defeat them. You could tell me anything suspicious they hear in the bazaar, their shops."

He stroked his beard, paused a long time before responding: "We Jews live isolated in ghetto of the old city. Most make and sell gold jewelry. Never get involved with Christian or Arab politics. But . . . I will talk with the Rabbi.

Some of us do have contact with gentiles – the Sultan does not forbid it. So, God willing, maybe we will see."

Three days later a short, elderly Jew with scissor blades sticking out of his pant's back pocket came to the consulate door looking for the American woman. He would speak to no one else. Telling the guard he was a tailor did not help. The guard called Browne who brought April to the door.

The tailor removed his black skullcap, looked both ways to insure no one nearby, slowly and softly said "I was cleaning this suit. I have the best customers, this suit it is a very expensive one. Made to Measure of imported wool, not local cheap cloth. And the man, he is very important, in the Italian Consulate."

April looked at Browne.

"Patience," he said.

"This paper is very fine quality. In inside breast pocket of jacket it was. You see those pockets are safer than ones flapped outside."

"Yes yes, I see. Go on."

"The letter from the Judge, it is not very long. It says something about he should give money to pay an important Swiss architect who is his spy; he has some German messages about an American invasion. Whatever that means. And the consulate should give the Judge money for the spy. Is that important?"

Browne wished the tailor had brought the letter.

April was ecstatic. She had the first link in her espionage chain.

Chapter Eighteen

The Russian Colonel's stone face concealed his unease.

Sergey Suronov, Director General of the GRU, Army Intelligence Branch, had transmitted this priority assignment, his most urgent, to this Tangier Consulate attaché. Because of its extreme urgency, the consulate Colonel presumed the request had been generated by Joseph Stalin himself and not by some Moscow apparatchick. The message purported to be military but he sensed the communist Secretary General's purpose to be more geopolitical. The telex had been terse:

America will soon invade Morocco. Troops may proceed east through Rif area to attack Rommel forces. Important know response of area guerilla forces. Which will they attack, American invaders or Vichy French defenders? Assess and report situation.

Colonel Pyotr Morensky considered the situation volatile. Nonetheless, he surmised that Stalin hoped the answer would be the French. In which case Hitler might be provoked to send an army through Spain to aid the French.

The result? He, military agent on the scene, was at risk.

The Colonel was not worried about personal danger. Although he and Tangier spies were well aware that with the exceptions of Sir Walter Harris, *London Times* correspondent, and Ian Perdicaris, shady accumulator of peasant lands, no foreigners who penetrated the Rif Mountains emerged alive. And those two exceptions had paid large ransoms.

It also was common knowledge that mountain people were Berbers, Caucasians who migrated there thousands of years ago. Unlike Arabs, they often had small noses, blue eyes and survived as fierce independence fighters. They treated captured garrison fighters harshly. Their favorite treatment was tying an enemy's hands with his bowels, dousing his legs with kerosene and lighting a match.

Colonel Morensky worried because in his military judgment such operation, a major rebel assault on either the Americans or the French was a silly idea. But what if it truly was Stalin's idea?

Ali Tassels sat listening on a mound of rugs.

His small shop was located in an old fondouk converted into a bazaar. Not since war began in Europe in 1939 had tourists come to his shop in the City of Tetouan near the Mediterranean Sea. The locals bought their rugs directly from weavers. He didn't care.

Agents of other countries knew the role of a merchant was his cover, that he was a General, leader of the Abd el-Krim guerilla forces.

To them all, he said: "El-Krim is old, retired. Now I buy weapons and supplies for our brave forces in the Rif. Spanish troops of General Orgaz or the French of General Noguès will never conquer our guerillas in the Rif."

The Tangier Option

Once again General Tassels listened to the same story. He politely offered Colonel Morensky a glass of mint tea and for himself rolled a cigarette, his mixture of cannabis fragments and coarse tobacco. He was mellow but in full possession of his wits. Last week that German agent Harry Daoud, the strange one in his white jellaba, had congratulated him on continued resistance against the Spanish by his Berber tribes. He encouraged him to do the same to the Americans if they came. But Daoud had come empty handed except for one 7.92 Mauser rifle, a token gift.

And now here sits this Morensky nosing around, praising him, suggesting he is the same as a GRU agent, saying that tribal communal living is much like communism. What this Russian spy really wants to know is what would Rif tribes do when the Americans came. If the invaders kick out the Spanish and French, could Russians move in?

Fingering Morensky's gift of a TT-33 Tokarev-Tula semiautomatic pistol, Tassels asked how many submachine guns would be given to arm his fighters.

The Russian offered only vague promises.

Tassels scattered cigarette remnants on the floor. "It is time to close shop," he said to the Colonel. "I must get an early start tomorrow morning for our Berber fortress high up in the Rif."

The early morning air was cool and smooth. A mist had burned off and now not one white puffy cloud floated in the blue September sky. This would be April's first experience in a small airplane. She trusted him without question but during the takeoff from Tangier sat by his side fists clenched and knuckles shining white. Then, after he throttled back, leveled off, and the engine racket diminished, she relaxed. The sensation of being aloft, not completely enclosed with the plastic side window flapped down, was glorious.

What freedom! She began to understand his passion for flying.

The airplane zoomed over green and gold rolling countryside, but to Jack the dark, looming terrain of the rugged Rif to starboard looked more intriguing. He began to dazzle April with the fun of diving into a valley only to soar up and around a sheer mountainside. It felt almost, but not quite like a roller coaster. Her mouth, wide open at first, soon was all smiles and her long hair waved in the wind. He wondered if it was the novel aerial experience or his expert flying that enraptured her. He wasn't sure which. Either way, she had grit.

The engine sputtered. Time to switch gas tanks from empty to full. He turned the fuel selector valve to 'reserve'.

The engine quit.

Ali Tassels, now cloaked in his tribal burnoose with its coarse, brown cowl over his head, had ridden his stallion into the mountains to meet a group of his tribesmen. He had heard the far off buzzing, seen the speck grow large in the sky. When the sound overhead abruptly ended he stared, then kicked his horse to a gallop.

Jack lowered flaps and set up a controlled glide while checking both countryside for a field and his instruments. Strange. The fuel gauge read full on the reserve tank. Quickly, he decided his options, selected a possible landing site. The only one without rocks was the small brownish field in a nearby valley.

He glanced at April, noticed her smile had disappeared. In what he hoped was an encouraging tone he said "Tighten your seat belt and hang on." Losing altitude, he soon saw the field consisted of rows of harvested plant stalks. He banked slightly to align the wheels with the furrows, tugged back the joystick, got the nose up, felt the airspeed bleed off and just before it stalled made a perfect three-point landing.

Immediately the front two wheels snarled in the tough vegetation. The tail rose in slow motion until the airplane, tilting to a 45-degree angle, came to rest on its front wheels and aluminum propeller.

"Damn," he muttered. "Not again."

"Nice landing," April said.

Jack shouted: "Get out before she burns."

But it didn't. When he smelled and tasted the fluid in that full tank it was water. He knew. Goosen again.

Sitting on a wheel, nursing an ankle sprained when she jumped, April suddenly pointed. Jernigan looked up. Silhouetted against the sky was a Moor on a big horse. The black hole of a military rifle was pointed at him.

Jack forced a grin. "American." He put his hands up.

The Moor lowered the rifle's muzzle. Now it pointed at his kneecap, not his head.

Tassels dismounted warily after Jack and April introduced themselves as diplomats at the Tangier Consulate. Gun beside him, he made tea and mulled what to do with these intruders. He was not in a hurry.

Jack restrained himself. He had learned that unlike Americans, these people have a different sense of time. And this mountain man had introduced himself as a merchant. If true, maybe he would barter for their lives before any decision was made. But he carried a rifle, not sales goods.

April broke the silence. In Arabic, she told Tassels she and her friend were merely flying to see the Rif mountains. Her Arabic surprised and impressed Tassels.

"We are near my town of Chefchaouen," he said. "I take you there. I have a short wave radio. Then, you contact your people and I will know exactly who you are, what to do with you."

April, limping, cheerfully responded: "I'm hungry, lead the way." She hoped she could charm their way to freedom.

For an hour or more the road was little better than a donkey path climbing between jagged rocks until the surprised captives entered, nestled amidst mountains, a sunken village plaza. It was a cobbled marketplace surrounded on three sides by shops and outdoor tea stalls. On the fourth side, loomed a massive fortress. At its base, Berber women squatted on colorful woven mats, selling green and red vegetables and mounds of white goat's cheese. All wore the same straw hats from which hung red woolen pompoms.

They followed Tassels down stone steps that ended at a heavily iron-studded door in a high wall. It did not look promising. Inside however, it opened to reveal a U-shaped structure with many rooms at two levels around an atrium. Tassels showed them to chambers, promising: "I will radio. After prayers we talk. If you are what you say – if not, ah."

It was evening before the three squatted cross-legged in silence around a low circular table and with their right hand fingers scooped lamb and couscous from a large brass tray. Jack and April looked for some sign. Were they captives or guests? Nothing. Tassels gave no sign. At last he began talking as a servant brought a basin of water for them to wash their hands.

"For centuries Chefchaouen was a holy city. Not long ago if you came here *your* throat would be cut, or worse." He nodded at April.

She shivered, turned to Jack who mustered a wink despite his own fears.

"Yet, if you had *Baraka,* the good luck, Abd el-Krim would only shoot you.

Jack cleared his throat. "We are not your enemy. Tell me about your Krim."

Tassels, sizing him up, wondering could this intruder be of use to his own cause, said "In 1920 our leader made this place his headquarters. Much later I became his General. He made me advisor and negotiator to get weapons from foreigners although he had little money to buy. My meetings were always in Tetouan, never here. You two are first foreigners permitted in this house. It is now mine. You," his forefinger jabbed at April, "leave us. Only men talk."

April resisted making a face.

Hoping they were now safe, Jernigan stretched his legs while Tassels was handed the mouthpiece of a water hookah, its bowl filled with glowing crushed leaves.

"Your aeroplane," he exhaled . . . "it is military is it not?" Sweet smoke wafted over them.

Jernigan, wishing for a Lucky Strike or Camel, fished a crumpled Galoise from his shirt pocket and said, "Yes," hoping that was the right answer. Then he added: "Tell me about this Chefchaouen of yours."

Tassels' eyes narrowed. "Spanish did not know this place existed until one of *their* aeroplanes flew over this valley. You must know that we Berbers struggled for years to chase invaders from our lands. But we did not have mortars or machine guns. France did. Spain, Franco did. And now you Americans do."

Jernigan knew that wasn't the reason for their defeat. Holcomb had briefed him on the Moroccan way of fighting. "Arab tribes have no strategy," he said. "When they find a small band of enemy soldiers each man, acting on his own, shoots wildly from a horse galloping at top speed, causes what damage he can, then goes back to his village."

Holcomb had chuckled, "Now it's a cultural thing mimicked in the cities with pride and rifle blanks are used instead of bullets. All for tourists, of course. It's called a Fantasia."

Jernigan changing the subject, ventured: "Tell me about Franco, General Orgaz, too. Do you think your people will ever be free?"

Tassels gave a snort. "Franco that *hombre poquito*. Yes, a man shorter than even we Berbers. He comes here a Captain. We make him fight hard and long to become a Colonel, leader of Spanish Foreign Legion. He spreads terror. When he wins a fight against us, his men return to barracks with our heads stuck on bayonets. He drove Krim, our leader, into retirement in our mountains. Then, in Spain, King Alfonso made Franco a General." Tassels spat on the floor.

"During the Spanish Civil War?"

"Tassels glared, held the hookah near his lips. "You know not much history." He sucked the mouthpiece in silence for a minute or two then shook it at his captive.

"Republicans in Spain exiled King Alfonso, so Fascists attack. Franco came back to the Rif to take command of his Army of Africa. Took this Spanish Legion across the Strait to fight those called communists. He called himself Generalissimo. That was not enough. He became El Caudillo. He thinks he is El Cid. That hero was worshiped. This man is feared as dictator. Yes, he is daring. Cunning too. So he exiled General Orgaz here."

"Why?"

"People say because Orgaz, Loyalist Spaniard, wants to restore Monarchy . . . I think it is to keep fighting us. Our men are brave, not afraid to die. Our fight is different, not European one."

"How so?"

The pause was smoke filled. "You have heard of the Istiglal?"

Jernigan could not pronounce it, let alone know its meaning.

"Nationalist Party. Independence party formed in city of Fez. I am now leader." Tassels eyes glowed with passion as he said: "We want French and Spanish colonial masters out. *Inshallah,* God willing our Sultan will be back from exile. Of course money helps."

Jernigan made an obvious gesture of looking at the rich furnishings around them.

Tassels shrugged. "One must live. These are Black Market, natural way of life. Berbers go down mountains; their donkeys carry cannabis in goatskin under figs and garlic. We also sell sweet oil. You call it olive oil. Make soap from it."

Jack knew of that scarcity. The soap at his pension was like a brown pebble.

"Some become drug runners, small bundles of hash. Each sells for three hundred dirham at the Café de Paris."

A very practical man, Jernigan thought. Even with mountain people where there is politics, money talks. He hoped Tassels would continue talking and provide him with information. "Who are these foreigners who come to see you? What do they want?"

Tassels spoke slowly. "Germans. Three days ago in Tetouan one who calls himself Daoud promised much. Said when Herr Hitler brings his army down through Spain into Morocco we in Rif will be friends. Live free of fear from Spanish."

"You don't believe that for a moment, do you General?"

Tassels eyes glittered. "Now people say Americans invade Morocco. If Berbers do not fight you, if we help you, what will you do for us?"

Jernigan was stunned by his abruptness. This Tassels was trying to barter – as if he was buying a rug. After a moment, he said, "General, Americans are not colonial rulers. I work for the consulate in Tangier, We have no weapons to give but do have money for our friends. This would be honorable money, friend to friend, not my ransom. Tell me how much and I will talk to my superiors. Let me use your radio."

When the mist on mountain slopes had burned off, Jack and April were free to wander in the sunshine. Without transportation or a guide they would not get far.

She grasped his hand and they strolled first around the plaza, admiring crafts and smiling to the Berbers who stared at them. Outside the town wall and across a deep valley, they saw a file of white clothed women coming downhill from a small square building capped with a white plaster dome. Jutting from a rod on its top was a black iron crescent that looked like a weather vane. It did not revolve.

In the Rif Mountains, Berbers of many tribes differ in their tongues, all unwritten and without alphabet. When queried, one of the women who spoke a smattering of Arabic answered April: "That building? The *koubba* of a *marabout* – a holy one."

April translated for Jack. "She's telling us it's a holy place, the tomb or shrine of a saint."

"Women go pray, for husband, for babies . . . " The woman ran out of words.

April started to walk beside a stream that coursed downhill and Jack followed. The air was crisp, fragrant from burning wood and charcoal. Large gray clouds began to form overhead. They soon came to a glade, stretched out on grass eaten short by sheep. Jack told April about his conversation with Tassels and April giggled telling him of a funny experience with the women in the *hammam*, the place where they took her to bathe. Jack laughed too, and then suggested they have a look in that shrine – now that all the women had left.

April hesitated. "If Tassels finds us there – "

The structure's stonewalls had no door. Jack had to bend before entering the one unfurnished room, dim without windows or candles. The silence was mysterious, intimate.

Jack looked at her, whispered: "You feel anything, getting any vibes?"

"A tingle – "

"That's all? Jack ran his hands over her breasts, felt her nipples rise. He pulled her body close and kissed her neck then lips with passion.

She breathed a heavy sigh. "You are no saint."

They sank to the hard earthen floor. He took her with the immediacy of a dam bursting under pressure.

Afterward, staring at the ceiling, Jack confronted her: "You didn't come to Morocco just to write a gossip column. Why?"

Angered, April abruptly sat up, studied the face she had so recently cupped. Leaning back down on an elbow she confided, "I shouldn't tell you this but I've wanted to since that night at the Continental."

Jack listened in growing amazement as April spoke of her cipher work at the consulate. When the torrent of words slowed, he leaned over and kissed her forehead. "My turn. I have something to tell *you*."

As Jack spoke of his role in the Navy and revealed his mission from the Admiral, the room grew darker. Before he had finished talking a thunderclap accompanied a sluice of rain that obliterated the hut's opening.

Now the lengthy mating was of two lovers, his hands caressing her breasts, her wide generous mouth sliding down his chest and belly to his groin, their murmurs of satisfaction.

Chapter Nineteen

Lieutenant Colonel Eddy pushed away sheets of scribbled notes. That left leg had a cramp again.

Things were not going well. The difficulty was not vice-consuls or any other agents he was running. That was straightforward espionage. He knew how to do it, control it. Any one failure there didn't matter all that much. But this planning for Torch was big time and created a whole new ballgame. General Donovan wanted counter-intelligence, deception plans to help conceal the invasion; told him he was the man on the scene. What could be a suitable Plan of Action?

Eddy pondered. With his amateur resources what sort of plan could he create that might match exploits – the daring-do – of the British? Imagine their blowing up the Baku Oilfields or the Iron Gates of the Danube River and interrupt the supply of Rumanian oil to the Germans.

Here in Morocco local resistance groups were no help. Eddy felt he couldn't trust any of them including 'The Five'. Wanting to foment sabotage when the invasion came, they said they had a new idea . . . these Jews neither know explosives nor was their scheme a useful one.

Again Eddy mulled another scenario; the one Browne came up with. He was running this Sheik, code named Mr. Strings, who was a saint to thousands in the radical Brotherhood. Browne proposed Mr. Strings call for a violent *jihad* against the French before the invasion. But a *jihad* could backfire on the Allies.

Eddy sighed. He was stuck with his own idea, a hairy scheme that could founder on execution. So who was available or skilled enough to execute such a mission?

Then his thoughts shifted to this matter at hand – Jernigan. He had received reports on the Tassels Affair from other sources and at first been incredulous. He expected high jinks from the amateur vice-consuls, not from a naval officer. Hard to believe one of his cadres had actually taken a military aircraft to give a woman a joyride.

And crashed!

What's more, not just any woman – my OSS cryptographer. He shuddered thinking of the security damage if she had been captured by the Nazis and tortured.

However, on reflection, he began to admire Jernigan's boldness, his skill in surviving that bloodthirsty Berber, Tassels. Pilots were much like marines, indifferent to danger. Rash. Crazy. Maybe he is just the man for my new idea.

In the outer office meanwhile, Lieutenant Jernigan had been pacing back and forth, ignoring Miss Pettigrew's smiles, rehearsing several explanations in his mind. Each sounded inadequate.

When she heard Eddy's buzzer sound, the pretty brunette advised Jack to not speak first.

Jack's usual confidence and high spirits dropped as low as his shoes when he entered Colonel Eddy's office and saw his cold glare. Standing in a brace, he launched into his lengthy rehearsed story about General Tassels and possible cooperation.

Colonel Eddy cut short Jack's account and the promises made. He took his time lighting a fresh cigar. Over the flame of a Zippo lighter emblazoned with marine insignia, he said, "We are at war. I could send you back to Norfolk; recommend a court-martial. Your Admiral might not put you in the brig; on the other hand, you could lose your commission. Is that not so? How would your father like that?"

Jernigan's face paled; eyes flashed. There was a moment of complete silence. Through his teeth he said, "Sir. There was no damage to the airplane, just a propeller nick. I know how to fix it. You take a round file and – "

"Stand at ease Lieutenant." Eddy rolled the cigar in his mouth, studied the glowing end. "You have another, a different option." He puffed the cigar.

Jernigan's eyebrows shot up. "Sir?"

"My Tangier OSS office controls numerous assets. The Germans have probably blown the cover of each including you. So what is needed here is a new face for counter-intelligence, a double agent. Someone I can trust who can pretend to be a disgruntled Nazi sympathizer, one to play a difficult role. Lieutenant, that could be you."

Jernigan was incredulous, his face showed it.

"Yes, such assignment is very dangerous."

"Sir, that's not it. I mean – I am not qualified. I wouldn't know what to do."

"Agreed. You are inexperienced, untrained." Eddy didn't add he was also somewhat bullheaded.

"You would disappear. We Americans have an Assessment Camp with British instructors and handbooks modeled on the MI.6 course for assets. There, you would be shown articles that aren't safe to touch. You will see explosive loaves of bread, fountain pens that squirt cyanide, booby trapped dung that are heaps made of explosive plastic painted to resemble feces."

Jernigan stood mute.

"You will also see and ignore any attempt to train you in invisible ink, microdot film, and sharpened point umbrellas . . . any of that claptrap. Your purpose there would be to go through physical training like a marine in order to handle yourself in dangerous, unexpected situations; become tough and skilled enough to climb walls; cope with close combat; do whatever needs doing to an enemy agent -- You do volunteer for camp and an urgent mission soon as you return, don't you?"

"Yes Sir."

"Good man. When you resurface you will have one less stripe. Temporary of course. I will leak you have been punished for that joyride escapade of yours."

Jernigan's first thoughts were why didn't the Colonel give the mission to Browne or to Holcomb – and was it a test? Then he understood; he was expendable.

"Sir, after this, uh, urgent assignment, then what happens?"

"You wait. Won't be long. Some enemy agent will contact you."

Jernigan's jaw twitched. "Yes Sir."

Eddy's eyes twinkled. "And Lieutenant, don't tell Miss Kearfoot."

After leaving Eddy's office, Jernigan went looking for Goosen. First he pulled the Colt from its belt back holster, removed then slammed the clip back into the butt, checked to see a round in the chamber. That Nazi was not in any of the watering holes – not at Madame Porte's, not in the Rif Hotel, nowhere to be seen. In the cold drizzle of a very early October rain, trench coat collar turned up, Jack depressed walked across town, from the bright boulevards of Mohammed V and Pasteur to the dark Avenue Antaki and his pension Omar el Khayyam.

The building's name had been a familiar one to April. She explained he had been an 11th century poet, famous for writing the *Rubaiyat*. She quoted one of her favorite passages:

The moving finger writes
And having writ moves on
Nor all thy piety nor wit shall lure it back
To cancel half a line

How true, Jack thought. You can't go back to what was before.

He walked briskly. His room beckoned with a half bottle of Fundador brandy. Soon he would have a charcoal blaze in the small fireplace.

Jack Jernigan was not a follower of the arts. As a child neither parent took him to museums; no girlfriend insisted on going to an art gallery. In America he had little interest in architecture; most buildings there seemed very ordinary. But in Morocco, wandering the boulevards and narrow streets by himself, he marveled at the buildings that varied from what he supposed was French or Spanish classical architecture to Moorish. His pension, only two stories tall but very wide, seemed to be a mixture of both. A wrought iron fence with ornate gate faced the street; behind it was a small garden. The two-story front, painted cream and an orange-yellow color, outlined the building's details: the rounded window tops and shallow balconies. The entrance projected forward, rose to a small third story with a short spire, where lived the owner.

Jernigan swung open the gate, sniffing the lush aroma of flowers whose names he did not know and unlocked the front door with a small iron key. The narrow tiled hallway between two formal salons with Moorish red banquettes led to the worn carpeted stairway in back. Jernigan climbed the stairs, entered the corridor to the left noting the hall's light bulb had burned out. At his door he hesitated. Was that the aroma of aftershave? Moroccan men never used it.

With his right hand Jernigan drew the Colt and pushed the safety forward with his thumb. With his left, he silently inserted and turned the key. He waited a full thirty seconds before pushing the door open. When he heard the faint squeak of the chair in the dark room, he dropped to the floor, rolled away and fired at a glimpsed figure. At the same time a cannon-like sound and a blinding flash of light knocked him unconscious.

Morning light flooded the room before Jernigan opened his eyes. A pulsing headache made him touch his head above his right ear. His hand came away sticky with blood. Rising slowly and looking sideways at the small mirror over the sink, he could see where the bullet had scraped a furrow through his scalp.

He searched the room looking for anything the assassin might have left behind. Maybe a cigarette stub or a book of matches printed with some name. The 9mm brass shell case on the floor in front of the cheap rattan chair was easy to spot. Harder to find was where his slug punctured old wallpaper. Searching on hands and knees, he spied something glittering behind a chair leg. He held it between his fingers. It was a gold flat toothpick. "Must have left in a hurry," he muttered.

Chapter Twenty

The Spanish Consulate, administrator of the Spanish Protectorate of Tangier, sponsored *the* social event of the year.

The proceeds of this Ball on October Fifth, a Friday, would go toward restoration of the *Gran Teatro Cervantes*, the old theater located to the southeast of the old city's Grand Socco. It boasted a magnificent Art Deco façade, intact as were the tiers of ornate patron boxes inside. Unfortunately, the rest of the interior had become a shambles. Recently, shabby seats with cigarette holes had been removed, blackened light bulbs replaced and the carpet cleaned for this major event. All the fascist elites from Spain, Occupied France, Germany and Italy had been invited. One of those representing Vichy France was Henri Foucauld.

Lieutenant Colonel Foucauld hated these social events. Not that he was unpopular. The wives of generals invited him to each and every social function after his young wife died in childbirth; his family and military credentials were superb. He was attached to the staff of Vichy General Charles Noguès who, never appearing at social affairs, preferred Foucauld to serve as his military representative. Now Henri stood at one of the long tables, festive with flowers and laden with tapas and Spanish wines. On stage, the Spanish band that played Saturday nights at the Hotel Rock on Gibraltar was swinging Benny Goodman's tune 'Sweet Georgia Brown'.

He regarded with distain the Spanish women wearing glittering necklaces and bracelets, their men in dress uniforms and the many French chests covered with medals. These were shameful medals. Awarded in defeat, as had been his grandfather's and his father's.

Somewhere, at some point, Henri had realized he was wasting his time, his honor. He wanted not to become another French superior officer who again would lose to the Germans as happened in 1870, 1914 and the 1940 blitzkrieg through Holland, Belgium and France.

Such humiliation. Such shame.

When the Germans formed the Vichy puppet government in Occupied France, led by that cabal of traitors, General Pétain as President, Laval as Prime Minister and Admiral Darlan, head of Armed Services, Foucauld requested transfer to Algeria. He had heard good things about the superior officer there, General Hubert Lyautey. Although a known homosexual, he was very effective in not only putting down guerilla activity, but also in bringing good roads and French culture to the populace.

Instead, Foucauld got Morocco.

Here in Tangier he felt himself useless and facing few military problems. His sole responsibility was training the Spahi, the native soldiers – spotless in white turbans and baggy pantaloons, red capes and knee high boots – to become an effective fighting force. Now, he had to question even that.

The Tangier Option

Fight against whom? It was no secret that the Americans were coming. He had met a young American explorer, a pilot who had actually asked him what would he do? Which side was he on? And many young officers talked in guarded tones at the French Officers Club. Would he become one with the group of officers committed to cooperation, not resistance, with the American forces?

Those officers knew their conservative superiors would obey the orders of Pétain and Darlan to resist. The young officers would not. That was a certainty. Foucauld was torn. He thought of the disgrace to his family's honor if he disobeyed a direct command. Uncertain, he had adopted an evasive but watchful demeanor with his peers.

He noticed the pretty American girl was talking to the Italian Consul General, the Duke of Bodiglio.

Although intending to speak with her, the chubby, simpering daughter of General Orgaz waylaid him.

Now, out of the corner of his eye, he saw that Dutchman Goosen grab the American girl's arm. He was smiling while leading her away. *"Merde!"* They were headed backstage. Goosen, that spy.

He started after them. Hesitated. Goosen would make a scene, or maybe the young woman would if she really was after some tidbit of gossip for her column. Was he ready to get overtly involved on behalf of an American?

In rapid strides he left the large theater.

The bitch. Now he had her. Goosen tightened his grip, still talking while pulling her along.

"Hey, take it easy," April grated. "This can't be all that important."

Inwardly, he was gloating. General Schellenberg had given him free reign including murder, saying, "This cipher clerk – give me everything she knows."

Never before had Goosen seen the General with jaw so hard, eyes so small. It was not only the Germans; the whole town was jittery. Everyone knew the Americans were coming. The Abwehr and the Schellenberg's SS needed to know much more. Each wanted to be first to Hitler with the all-important specifics: Where? When?

Goosen whispered to April, "I've got something secret for your newspaper, your eyes only. We will go backstage where no one will hear."

"If this is so secret, where did you hear it?"

"General Auer, but all that later. Come this way." He led her behind the thick velvet curtain and a scrim painted with Don Quixote on his mule, lance pointed at a windmill.

"This better be good."

Backstage was a clutter of scaffolding and used paint buckets. Ropes to hoist flies hung from a metal walkway above.

Goosen's charming smile vanished. With his hands on her shoulders he pushed her backward onto a paint-spattered chair.

"Hey!" She yelled.

From behind a painted wood flat two burly men appeared, grabbed her arms and held her immobile.

Goosen sneered. "My friends never are gentle with women. Hot Cat, better for you to sit and listen. Of course if you scream we will gag you, tie you up."

The Tangier Option

April was stunned that he knew her code name. Wide-eyed and tense, she shrank away as Goosen thrust his face so close she could smell the beer he had been drinking.

In a threatening tone that chilled her bones, he continued: "I have only two questions for you: At what place will your American troops land and on what date? The Abwehr already know, want it confirmed. You are the American cipher officer. You do the decoding. You know; tell me. Now."

April stared at the man standing with his arms crossed before her. He was out of his mind. Those secrets had not been leaked to the best of her knowledge. Regardless, she would never talk. Her mouth clamped so shut her teeth ached.

Goosen's strong impulse was to rip off that dress that clung to every curve of her body, expose those magnificent breasts. Never before, not even in South Africa had he seen a woman tortured. Watching it happen to this beautiful body would be exciting. The pulse in his neck throbbed. Not yet, he told himself; later, after she spills her guts.

"My General knows most details of the Allied invasion forces, their size, which harbors in the US and Scotland they will sail from." He didn't add, "Our wolf pack of three hundred submarines waits in the Atlantic, at the opening to the Strait." Instead, he said, "I only want the date and place of attack." He bent, took her hand and kissed the clenched fingers.

She recoiled. "Never. Never!"

139

"You will be on the winning side, a hero, given a chateau in France, Switzerland or wherever you wish." His taut face was earnest, but she could not mistake the madness in his eyes.

How could she have been so charmed by him before? With his muscular body arched over her, he looked like a coiled cobra about to strike. April wrenched her hand away, tried to jump up. He slapped her face so hard she felt a welt rising.

"Sit and listen," he commanded. "I do not want to gag and tie you. Understand?"

April nodded, determined never to crack no matter what he did.

"I can take you to a remote place where you will be tortured. It might take hours. You will want to be resolute. Eventually you will cry out for mercy."

"No. Never."

This woman is tough, he thought. He paused, tried a different tactic.

"At my command," he said, "your American pilot will be captured. You two will be transported to a place no one here can find. You will watch the Gestapo give your lover's testicles electric shocks, his fingernails pulled out. But that is only the beginning. He will collapse; he will be revived. You will feel his intense pain as we first smash one kneecap then the other, crush both testicles."

Tears came. April shuddered.

"Of course, he may not know the answer. But you do and you will talk. Better you save him that agony." He shrugged, still pretending to care for her. "I don't want this any more than you do, but I cannot stop the SS specialists from doing their job. Only you can."

Through her tears April said yes, she would tell him everything she knew. She gulped for breath, tried to control herself while Goosen stood over her, menacing. Then she spoke in short spurts: "The date . . . it is December ten . . . and the place . . . south. Dakar, on the West African coast." She slumped in the chair.

Another sharp burning slap to the face jarred her upright. "So easy? You sell out so easy? Come, my dear, I am not so easily fooled."

Goosen heard loud voices heading toward the backstage area. So did April. Her mouth opened to cry out but a thug thrust in a gag and tied a cloth over her face.

Goosen growled, "Put her in the car. *Schnell.*"

Jernigan did not know what to make of Foucald's sputtered message. He had just ordered his usual martini at the Minza while waiting for April. But the French Officer's heavy breathing from his sprint uphill and his obvious anxiety spurred him to action.

Pushing past evening strollers, running downhill three blocks he heard, a half-block ahead, the wail of a Goodman clarinet reaching the highest note of 'Sing Sing Sing', stopping and a drummer launching into the famous Gene Krupa drum solo. That was when he caught a glimpse of April, kicking and struggling, being tossed head first into a black Mercedes.

Damn. He vaulted a railing, ran toward the auto that had begun to move, its open doors closing. Two red taillights vanished before he could catch up panting and cursing. Around the corner Jack saw a man getting into a

Citroen 2-CV. He sent him sprawling with a shove, grabbed the fallen keys and started the engine. His scalp pressing against the canvas roof's underside, he swung the little white car around and up the street in pursuit.

Uphill south to Boulevard Pasteur, he followed the Mercedes onto the Place de France roundabout with its adjacent Café de Paris. He circled it ignoring the screeching of brakes and honking of horns from other cars. He saw the Mercedes turn left, tried to follow, got caught between a taxi, delivery truck and a string of cars. Now nothing was moving. To the astonishment of tea drinkers, he drove the CV onto the Café sidewalk knocking over chairs and tables. He figured Goosen must be headed northeast up the Old Mountain where rows of German villas with high walls could hide him. No. The red taillight was speeding downhill again, headed for the port.

All this time, April sat bouncing on the back seat jostled between the two Germans while Goosen sat in front beside the driver. When the Mercedes hit a pothole and sideswiped cars parked on the narrow streets, she had taken off the cloth and spit out the gag. Now she watched in horror as each thug drew a Mauser pistol from his waistband and pointed it out his rolled down window.

She twisted to see out the rear window, saw in the semidarkness a small white car following them. Their shots missed – too much swerving and bouncing by both cars.

The Mercedes drove through the port's open gate without stopping, onto the long concrete pier. At its end, Goosen abruptly pulled April out of the car. The harbor's revolving beacon briefly shone on a small trawler alongside the pier. Its inboard engine was idling.

"My God," she gasped, "You're taking me out of Morocco!"

Goosen pulled struggling April toward the boat.

She looked back at the white car, recognized Jack getting out. Bullets shattered his windshield, splattered concrete near him.

Jack will die! What could she do?

She wrenched free, ran to the pier's edge and dove off into ink black water.

The white beam of the harbor beacon came around again. Goosen looked down into the bayside water, grabbed a thug's Mauser and shot off the clip into the widening ripples.

Bubbles surfaced.

Three port guards came running and shouting: "Stop. Stop."

Goosen and the two Germans jumped into the trawler. It roared away into darkness.

Jack, running to where he had last seen April leap into the water, dived in.

He saw nothing . . . could touch nothing.

He surfaced, dove again and again and again.

Harbor debris clinging to his body and wet clothes dripping and stinking, Jack was not in the mood to explain his appearance at his apartment. The Continental was nearby, just up the hill. In its narrow lobby, the porter slept soundly in a chair across from the vacant concierge counter. Jack went up the twisting stairway and down the creaking corridor to April's door.

From the darkness a voice said: "What took you so long?"

He threw his wet clothes beside hers on the floor and climbed into bed.

She had bathed. She was hot.

Chapter Twenty One

It was midday when Captain Browne strode into the code room. "I have bad news," he said looking tired and disgusted.

April pushed aside her codebook, Stork looked into his coffee cup where only dregs remained.

"Seems not only do the Germans monitor our transmissions to vice-consuls, they have broken the code."

"Oh no." April reddened. "How do you know?"

"Informer. Sorry April, it's not your fault. It probably goes back to when that charwoman was copying your files. Apparently the Germans got around to comparing your decoded messages to their intercepted messages, the coded ones. You will need to construct a new vice-consul code. I'll send out your new codebooks to all concerned."

April frowned in concentration. "Wait a minute. Weren't you talking with Jack, ah, Lieutenant Jernigan about . . . uh, sergeant would you mind making a fresh pot of coffee?"

Browne sat down in the sergeant's vacated chair. "Now –"

"I know I'm not supposed to be privy to what you and Jack talk about and I'm not, except, well, you *do* talk about needing to plan a deception. Here is a great opportunity for one."

"I'm listening."

"Why don't we write a string of messages using our broken code. The enemy will intercept, read and believe these false ones. Like about the invasion."

Browne grasped her idea right away. "Hand me that pencil, some paper too."

April leaned closer, pushed a lock of hair out of her face. "How about Dakar," she said. "Something simple and short that will get their attention . . . try this: Anticipate allied flotilla to attack Dakar."

He put down the pencil.

"You code it and I'll give it to my corporal on the MIDWAY set for Morse key transmission. The Germans have a radio in the town of Ceuta. German operators there will recognize his fist as authentic.

Jernigan felt discouraged. What a bummer.

He had come back from Assessment Camp cocky and ready for action, toughened by his daily twelve-hour arduous experiences. He was in top physical condition, self-confident in his new capability. Now, meeting in secrecy at the Colonel's villa high up the Old Mountain, it all seemed a waste of time and effort. No Axis agent had approached him. Eddy's double agent scheme seemed a fiasco.

Colonel Eddy crooked a finger and Jernigan followed him up a flight of outdoor stairs to a box-like structure on the roof. Inside were upholstered banquettes on three sides with windows above. Eddy eased himself into a wicker chair; left leg outstretched he watched his Lieutenant standing to admire the panorama of Spain, the Strait, Gibraltar and Tangier. "I often come here to do my thinking," he said. "Gives me perspective on my job. Within naked eyesight there are probably five thousand enemy agents out there, each and every one scheming how to harm America."

Eddy rubbed his brow. "You are now trained to be an effective counter- intelligence agent, but our problem is obvious. You are below their radar screen."

Jernigan felt sure the Colonel didn't summon him up here to talk doom and gloom. Eddy must have something up his sleeve.

Colonel Eddy waved him to a seat. "Listen carefully. As you guessed from the recon task the Admiral gave you, North Africa is going to be invaded. The Germans know this. Where and when it will happen they don't know. Now this next part is Top Secret, for your ears only. When the invasion occurs an important person will be in Tangier. If the Germans find out . . . without doubt their agents will attempt assassination." Eddy's eyes had a faraway look as though seeing a disaster. "Our job here is to forestall any Axis attempt on this person's life. I cannot tell you who he is. That comes later. But you can play a dangerous part in this scenario that misleads the enemy."

Jernigan nodded, eyes glowing.

"First thing is give you a higher profile, make you a credible double agent. Here is my Plan. You are bitter about our Navy. Your career is shot. You are willing to sell Naval Attaché secrets. And to demonstrate your new role's credibility, Jack, you are going to expose one of our OSS

147

secret operations. Browne and I have code named it STATIC."

Jernigan grinned. Colonel Eddy had called him by his first name.

Captain Browne drove his personal Studebaker up an unpaved road and parked beside a small local restaurant. Inside, several Moroccans clustered around one of the five tables. Browne chose the one in a corner. "Good place as any for talking," he said to Jernigan.

Without asking, the waiter brought a straw basket of flat, round slabs of whole grain bread and four small dishes: two with olives and toothpicks, two with spiced beet relish. Browne ordered grilled sole. "The sole here is fresh, big too. We'll split it."

After the waiter disappeared, Browne began: "Seems German submarines are very effective in the Strait." When his toothpick slid off an olive, he picked it up with his fingers, chewed around the pit. "As many as fifty percent of the Malta supply ships never make it. I'm damn sure a German radio in Spanish Morocco is tipping them off."

"How do you know?"

"An informer. You don't need to know who he is. This guy has tipped us off about an Axis lookout post operated by Germans. It's operating up the Med coast in the town of Ceuta. We have a dossier on that operation's honcho. He's a Spanish national, named Manuel Centano. He works for German intelligence. Gets three thousand pesetas salary every month and five thousand for expenses, Code name: Antonio."

Jack nodded, "Somewhere there's a reason you're telling me this."

"Right. Another important convoy is coming through very soon. Malta needs the foodstuffs. But British destroyer escorts are never effective enough. Their SIS Colonel here asked our Colonel to help prevent heavy losses, to eliminate this radio." Browne didn't add this would be retaliation for the Germans exploding a mail sack on the Gibraltar ferry, killing two British security guards.

"The drill is, you and me are going to do just that. Try these olives; the black wrinkled ones. Delicious."

Jack looked at him. "This German radio that's in the Spanish town – "

He paused, watched the waiter open a bottle of red wine for them, noticed it was a Cabernet from grapes grown in the Atlas Mountain foothills. With glasses filled and waiter gone, he asked: "When can we go there?"

"Touchy situation. Lieutenant General Orgaz told the British Colonel he doesn't believe Spanish Morocco harbors a German set. But we know those Spanish officers are fascists who work with Axis Intelligence."

"So what's the solution?"

"Orgaz agreed on the basis that one of his people goes on the raid too."

"Doesn't that mean Orgaz will blow the whistle, we'll have a reception committee?"

"That's why you will be first to leak the news, to the Germans."

The fish, indeed, was very good.

Chapter Twenty Two

That night Lieutenant Jack Jernigan appeared at the Rif Bar in uniform. The Benny Goodman style band was again blaring their passable rendition of 'King Porter Stomp'. General Auer's table was crowded with cronies and underlings. Jernigan walked past, making eye contact only with the fat man in the white jellaba, then taking a side table. His dry martini and Harry Daoud arrived at the same time. Jack motioned to a chair. Daoud stared at Jernigan's sleeve where a few threads lingered from a missing gold stripe.

"That bad? Airplane mishaps and gossip travel fast in this town."

Jernigan gulped half the martini, knew an opening when he heard one. "I have information that is not gossip."

The fat man leaned closer, his breath smelling of sausage, his eyes opaque. "You are selling?"

"Freebe."

"Freebe? What is that?"

"Means no charge. I look to a future relationship, one rewarding for me. You pass this along. Afterward we talk money."

"You Americans make a business of everything."

It was thirty-three kilometers northeast to the rocky promontory overlooking the harbor of Ceuta.

The house on the summit once white-stuccoed, was now stained and discolored with spreading vines. The raiders parked their two cars a hundred fifty yards downhill, on the side where the coastline fell into the open Mediterranean. Spanish Algeciras and British Gibraltar across the Strait looked within spitting distance. Browne and Jernigan got out of the Lincoln Zephyr, Holcomb and the Spanish Naval officer out of the Plymouth. The Plan called for two cars in case captives needed to be taken back to Tangier for interrogation.

The building appeared deserted. Browne, cradling a Thompson machine gun and Jernigan, with his Colt thrust forward, walked through the small garden to a sturdy looking front door. No one answered Browne's hammering of the brass knocker. Jernigan shot out the door lock and both men rushed in.

At the same time, a back door creaked open and a stout woman ran out. Holcomb grabbed her arm, spun her around. The Spanish officer recognized the woman. "This one is Frau Meyer, a cleaning woman. She knows nothing. Let her go." Lieutenant Holcomb wanted to give the Spaniard one on the jaw. Instead he kicked the woman's butt before she ran off and they entered the house.

For three hours, in two teams, the four men searched from top to bottom, tapped walls, moved aside tattered rugs to examine the floor and used its trap door to get to a cellar.

No radio.

Jernigan turned to Browne, "Would you mind leaving me the Plymouth? I want to stay awhile, enjoy the view."

He went up to the roof, sat on its parapet with his feet dangling over the side and stared across the water. It occurred to him that the transmitter need not be big or powerful to reach Spain.

The breeze freshened and he sniffed more than a whiff of salty ocean. It triggered more thoughts. He dashed down and out of the house.

The garden was not much to look at – patches of ground cover and a large clay pot sitting in a flowerbed. He drove his hand into the dirt. Nothing. He moved the pot a foot away. Loose dirt. With both hands, he shoveled until he saw the shiny top of a small aluminum suitcase.

Bingo.

Bouncing in and out of turbulent clouds in General Auer's Junker to a meeting with him, Chief of Abwehr Admiral Canaris tried to quell his nervous stomach. It wasn't fear of flying. It was the memory of yesterday's meeting with Hitler. The Führer had been more than irate – he was insane. Something surely must be done about that madman.

In his mind he relived that meeting in Bergonstadt. Hitler had several military chiefs present but not General Goëring who was excluded. Everyone knew Hitler was still unhappy with Goëring because of the loss of so many trained pilots in the Spanish civil war, the failure of the aerial Battle of Britain and now this: British Lancaster's bombed German soil every night and American B-17's bombed by daylight.

Hitler had begun the meeting by saying he wanted a plan that did not take away any military forces from Russia or Rommel or any other location. Then he said it was necessary to forestall or make politically impossible the coming Allied invasion of North Africa. And what was his brilliant Plan to be? He wanted a covert operation and gave us an option – assassinate Roosevelt or Churchill!

Monstrous.

Breaking a brief silence General Schellenberg had commented that Prime Minister Churchill was scheduled soon to travel to Gibraltar. Access to him on that heavily fortified rock might be difficult. When Himmler suggested it should be America not England where we should create confusion and disarray, emboldened Schellenberg added Roosevelt was going to Tangier, Morocco. Hitler decided saying, "The English are stalwart, Americans are soft."

When Canaris finally arrived in Casablanca at the German Armistice Commission's headquarters in the Miramar Hotel, General von Wulish in command met him with courtesy. Both were old-guard Prussian officers. Each knew the other had similar ideas about Hitler's conduct of the war that had to remain unspoken.

Wehrmacht Abwehr General Teddy Auer was not present. It seemed he was on his yacht at the harbor. Von Wulish remarked, "Goering takes Old Master paintings from Jews; Auer collects cases of champagne, Bugatti and Alfa Romeo race cars and now a yacht. Sometimes instead

The Tangier Option

of the Junker, he uses it to go up the coast to Tangier." Both men raised eyebrows then shrugged.

The one hundred twenty foot yacht with a large swastika fluttering at the stern was not difficult to find. General Auer received Canaris on deck, mentioned the boat had once belonged to a black marketer. He made the gesture of an index finger cutting a throat, grinned and said, "Now it is my castle. No one can intrude here. It makes for a secure place for work and I have my own radio and operator, also a chef. You are in time for a drink and lunch."

Canaris glanced at a glass case displaying curved jeweled daggers in silver sheaths and replied, "Perhaps later, first to business." The aristocratic admiral regarded with distaste this ruthless brute made General because of his thuggery.

Seated opposite each other at a round table in the comfortable aft lounge, Canaris revealed to the intelligence general Hitler's desire and expectation of an immediate Tangier Option. He bluntly put without further explanation: "Der Führer wants us to assassinate President Roosevelt."

With a lifetime career devoted to crime and murder, hardened Auer showed no surprise or emotion. He also knew better than to try and pump his boss for details of the Hitler meeting. "So, Admiral, a plan is needed?"

Canaris looked around, spoke softly. "In no way could we target President Roosevelt in America. However, intercepted transmissions tell us he will be traveling to Morocco, to Tangier."

"Seems a strange thing to do."

155

"Kings of yore led their armies in battle. Previously he traveled by battleship to meet with Churchill at sea. Now he comes not only to witness the expected invasion, but also to meet with the Sultan's Vizier. Presumably to make sure the Arabs do not revolt and make trouble when the Yankees invade."

"Yes, makes sense. Roosevelt likes to meddle, direct things himself."

"He must be our target. But," Canaris emphasized, "Luftwaffe bombing is out – Göering cannot be part of any plan. So, General," he lifted his hands, palms up . . . "what can be done locally?"

Always jovial, Auer expressed appreciation that Canaris had come to him for involvement in Hitler's plan and responded with an immediate idea. He knew of a Spanish neutral that burned for revenge against the French.

"His name is Paco Alvarez, a Count's son. He fought in General Orgaz' Spanish Foreign Legion against Berber tribesmen in the Moroccan Rif. You see this Alvarez is bitter because Spain, which conquered most of Morocco, lost the biggest part of its colony to France by an international Treaty. Der Führer will think our plan to use a Spanish assassin wonderful because blame will not fall on us. And success would force Franco to take the German side instead of fence-sitting."

The General did not think it appropriate to also mention this Alvarez was excitable. Recently, he had hit another car and when the driver called him 'stupido', had pulled a knife. Fortunately a police officer happened to come by and drew his gun.

Expressionless, Admiral Canaris meshed and studied his fingers on the table while pretending to consider the suggestion. Then he shook his head, dryly commented.

"Never use an amateur. I never trust an idealist, one who rushes ahead purely on political beliefs. Such an assassin has too many neuroses, uses unprofessional methods. In contrast, aerial bombing is aloof, technical, would be so much more efficient."

"Good point," Auer said and smiled while the hand in his lap clenched. "There is another way. I have an agent, an American Navy pilot who is disaffected. He wants to be of service to me . . . for money."

"General, in espionage, money makes for the best, the most careful agent. Contact this pilot. Keep me informed of progress but not details."

Chapter Twenty Three

USS Augusta
8:00 A.M. October 23, 1942

On the bridge of the eleven-year-old heavy cruiser, RADM Henry Kent Hewitt handed the warship's captain his sailing orders.

That officer previously only knew only he was to link up mid-ocean with two British flotillas - Center and Eastern Task Forces and the American Air Group after its training in Bermuda. Now he knew his ultimate destination. Moreover, ONI advised the admiral that the departure of his Western Task Force out of Hampton Roads, Virginia, likely had been telegraphed by spies to the enemy in Europe, then relayed to U-boats at sea.

Even so, Hewitt felt relieved to be at sea; smelling ocean breezes helped dissipate the tensions of the past several months – problems, pessimisms, doubts and endless conferences. General Eisenhower himself still thought this a suicide mission. No wonder. As recently as yesterday, at the 'final' conference this time in Norfolk, General George Patton in his usual lack of tact had said to him, "Never in history has the Navy landed an army at the planned time and place. Admiral, if you land us anywhere within fifty miles of Fedala-Port Lyautey and within one week of D-Day, I'll go ahead and win."

Nevertheless, Hewitt was filled with pride as he viewed the immense vista of the American armada at sea. In addition to cruisers, troop transports and cargo vessels with flanking destroyers, the October 28 rendezvous with the Air Group from its Bermuda training further enlarged the flotilla.

Scanning the horizon he could make out the USS Ranger and her four 'Sangamon' class of escort carriers converted from tankers and just out of the yards. They carried twenty-eight Grumman Avenger torpedo bombers, thirty-six Douglas dive-bombers and one hundred eight Wildcat fighter planes to escort the bombers. They also ferried seventy-six P-40 fighters for basing at Casablanca as soon as it was captured.

He had heard the rumors that aboard were so many raw pilots who had never made a carrier landing that Air Group leader RADM Mcwhorter was unwilling to risk their lives practicing en route.

Hewitt knew this Torch operation was like the early opening of the football season – a first league game without the team having had practice or getting all needed equipment. But there were exceptions. Word had gotten out about the good work of Lieutenant Commander Tommy Booth with his Red Ripper fighter Squadron on the Ranger. His pilots had been drilled in communications, enemy aircraft identification and fighter aerial combat. These tactics were based on the concept that an element of two pilots should fight as one unit rather than single plane attack as in World War One. Booth's young men were as sharp and eager as could be expected.

Hewitt also liked his flotilla's team spirit and humor. However, Rear Admiral Ike Giffens, leading the fleet on battleship Massachusetts, was outraged. He had radioed a message to the fleet saying: "The amount of useless chatter over the ship-to-ship radio telephone is disgraceful. It sounds more like a Chinese laundry at New Years than a fleet going to war. We are not training broadcasters." To which the commanding officer of the Wichita replied by flag signal, "Congratulations and good morning sir. In my opinion the Chinese laundry signal is the best I have seen so far."

Admiral Hewitt, now in command of the unified forces, had come a long way since he had been Captain of the USS Indianapolis in the mid thirties. Then, President Roosevelt used her as his 'Ship of State.' Now, aboard that same vessel, he was not made aware that Admiral Davidson and General Ernie Harmon had met on deck. Each carried the secret operations book, a seven hundred-page tome agreed upon in joint army/navy planning conferences. When these two officers discovered neither had understood nor read this Plan, as thick as a New York telephone directory, both books went overboard.

Meanwhile, far away in Madame Porte's bar, Jernigan was quietly nursing a martini, thinking about his private meeting earlier with the Colonel at his villa. To lose surveillance he had changed taxis twice, gone to the Tingis bar's toilet and out the back door. Eddy had been delighted with the success of the Ceuta mission, offered congratulations and one of his rare Havana Corona cigars.

"That no German radio technicians were at the Ceuta site," Eddy mused aloud, "proves our deception is working. Your double agent role has been proven."

Jack stubbed out his Camel cigarette. Where was the German contact? What was taking so long? Hey, he told himself, don't get so anxious.

Again his thoughts reverted to the meeting. Eddy had counseled: "Don't be impatient. It's not unusual for a spy to remain without contact for months. The Germans had moles in England who were unknown for years. When the Krauts have something important that is a fit for you, you will be contacted soon enough."

In the mirror, Jack saw the fat man enter the café, look around, make brief eye contact, then walk out. Jack pretended to turn his attention to the martini, waited a decent interval and followed Daoud.

Half a block behind, he tracked him downhill to a shabby waterfront café displaying no sign on its nondescript façade. He found him in back, in a small windowless room amidst stacked cases of French wine and cartons of American cigarettes.

Daoud seated in a rickety wooden chair greeted him with: "Black market stuff, old sod. We can talk here."

Jernigan stood with his back to the wall, pulled out and lighted a cigarette. Now he would find out what sort of dirty work this English mongrel had in mind.

Daoud gloated, seeing the shaved patch of skull with antiseptic stain above Jack's ear. From a slit in his long jellaba he produced the semiautomatic Mauser that had

The Tangier Option

produced the wound. With a muted chuckle he placed it on the crate of cigarettes beside him.

Jernigan put his hand in his pocket.

Daoud immediately picked up, pointed the Mauser.

Jernigan's hand emerged; put the gold toothpick on the case. "Expecting trouble?" he said, unbuttoning his jacket so the Colt's butt at his waist was visible. He was angry and tense, as tense as he'd ever been in Tangier.

A cynical smile formed on Daoud's fleshy lips. "In this business old sod, you never know." The renegade Englishman picked up his flat toothpick jabbed it for emphasis. "Things change overnight." Then he stuck and rolled it in the corner of his mouth.

Jernigan wasn't sure if that comment meant him, the black market or espionage. Through tight lips he grunted: "You want to talk; get to it."

"There is a very important man, one whom certain people want . . . assassinated."

Jernigan hoped his shiver didn't show. He inhaled then blew the smoke through pursed lips. "Why me? I'm not a professional killer and you have enough goons that can do the job."

"You will understand soon enough. This person will be in Tangier soon for a brief time; he will be well guarded. None of our people will be able to get within fifty yards of him. If I tell you the name and how you could do it, have you have any objection," he paused, "to *murder*?" He deliberately stressed the word.

Jack didn't like the sound of that at all. But this was the reason he was here. He must learn more. Besides, he was intrigued. Who could be so important? He ground out

163

the glowing cigarette with his heel. "What do you have in mind? If you have a way I think can be done, I will do it."

Daoud leaned forward, studied the Lieutenant closely for a reaction. This was the key moment. He whispered, "The one to be killed is President Roosevelt."

Jack's mind went numb. By instinct, keeping a blank stare, Jack fished for another cigarette, searched his pockets for his Zippo lighter. He was surprised his hands were so steady.

"And the way to do it is by air. He is coming to Morocco and will be housed in the American Consulate building. You bomb it."

No amount of 'cloak-and-dagger' training could have prepared him for this. At a loss for words again he inhaled, exhaled and watched the puff of smoke swirl away.

"Well old thing, what do you say?"

"Why don't your friends use an experienced bomber pilot? Some Nazi?"

Daoud chortled. "Thank you for the complement. We blokes are not privy to SS thinking. But I can guess that Germany does not want to start a war with neutral Morocco."

"The Consulate walls are very thick stone."

"How did you think we pulverized London. You will have one of those blockbusters."

Jernigan had to resist the urge to pull the Colt and shoot this bastard. He stared at the ceiling as though deep in thought, looked at his fingernails. "It can be done but it will be expensive."

"We will provide the aircraft."

"I want one hundred thousand U.S. dollars, half before and half after. Afterward, I will fly to neutral Spain. For sanctuary. Pay me the second half there."

The renegade spy's gaze locked on Jernigan's gray eyes. Not wanting to reveal triumph, with a fleeting scowl he said: "I think our people will agree."

Jernigan felt the urgent need to inform Eddy of this astonishing, this outrageous scheme, but pressed Daoud for more details before hurrying off.

The large jellaba shifted on the small chair. "Later. Later, old thing."

Soon as Jernigan departed, the back door opened; a military-looking man in civilian clothing strode in.

Daoud stood up, said, "Colonel, What do you think?"

The Waffen-SS Brigade staff officer was brusque. "Making progress." He did not mention that Reichsführer Himmler had adopted the Plan proposed by Admiral Canaris and General Auer but afterward reassigned it to Brigadeführer Schellenberg. Cautious, he did not trust Canaris and his Abwehr General.

Daoud pocketed his Mauser. "I doubt this American can do it."

"There is a fifty-fifty chance of success. No matter which way it goes the highest authority will know we tried, did our best."

"What happens next?"

"Your role is over. Don't speak of it to anyone including the American pilot. Others will attend to details."

Jack felt proud and in high spirits as he walked back up the hill. He had an incredible story, vital information to give to the Colonel. And he had handled that spy without any help. It wasn't until he reached the Minza that the full import of the plot hit him. He had agreed to collaborate, to be a killer for the Germans. Could he ever back out? No. He knew too much. What would happen to him? He doubted that Eddy or Browne would save him if things went wrong. He had dug himself into a hole.

At the Minza, Colonel Eddy wrote a telex message to General Donovan on the special encoding pad, tediously printing one capital letter in each gray printed square so that Assistant Cryptographer Hot Cat could insert the coded version into the empty space below each line.

The Muezzin was singing the pre-dawn call to prayer when Jernigan turned the key in the lock. First thing, he poured himself a half-tumbler of Fundador brandy and tossed it down. Next, he took a long shower; surprised to find hot water at that hour. He was still thinking about the long day, starting with the Daoud meeting and later with Eddy. The Colonel's attitude had been a surprise. Jernigan couldn't read Eddy's reaction to his debriefing until he saw him visibly relax in the chair. Instead of anger or dismay at his rash behavior, the Colonel had been extravagant with praise.

"Jack," he said, "You are a credit to the Navy and this office. Think of it this way. First of all and most important, we now know what the German leaders have in mind for Roosevelt. I will pass this vital news on to our

Consul, also to Donovan. Second, if you hadn't agreed to the assassination, Daoud's spymaster surely would have found some other pilot, perhaps a disaffected Spaniard or a French one to take the assignment. And third, in that event, either Daoud would have been told to use that Mauser or, more likely, an experienced assassin would have been sent to eliminate you."

The second surprise Eddy hit him with was his response to the question: "What should he do about it?"

"Nothing."

"Nothing at all sir?"

"You don't think the SS did that scene with you without having an ending to their game plan, do you?" Eddy didn't wait for an answer. "Soon as Roosevelt leaves for Morocco, they will want to spring the rest of their trap. That is when you will be taken to some airplane with a bomb."

"Then what do I do?"

"Good question." Colonel Eddy hoped Roosevelt would be made safe, wished he could say the same for the Lieutenant. He said casually, "Let's play that one by ear. But you know what you must do."

His expression changed and in a grim voice added: "Meantime, something else has come up."

Chapter Twenty Four

There was a wild east wind blowing off the Sahara that moonlit night.

In Morocco that dry wind is called the Levanter. The same wind that in the village of Arles, France drove Vincent Van Gogh to cut off his ear and had wives in Tangier putting rat poison in their husband's food.

Jernigan too, was depressed. The espionage training and physical toughening in Scotland, compressed from six weeks into three weeks, seemed useless. From what little he heard through the grapevine, father had been in a major sea battle. Here, he hadn't had a chance to use all that British training.

Then a late evening meeting at the Colonel's villa changed everything, sent his spirits soaring.

Eddy, standing at a window looking at the port below, surprised him by asking: "You know we have a radio run by Browne's signal corps corporal?"

"Yes sir." He also knew that the Consul had made Eddy move his radio to the villa on the Old Mountain. But he guessed the Colonel wasn't just making small talk. He figured this conversation would lead somewhere important.

"When the corporal isn't on station sending or receiving official messages, he likes to scan the spectrum of frequencies to see what else he can pick up. Recently he heard messages in German. I am led to believe that transmitter's function was to send coded instructions to U-boats in the Strait waiting for Allied shipping. We need to eliminate that transmitter before our invasion fleet gets here." He did not add that this secret operation would be so politically sensitive that General Donovan had to get him authorization from the President.

Jernigan, knowing better than to ask how soon the invasion would be, asked instead: "Colonel, does the corporal know the radio's location?"

"None of our informants say it is in Morocco. Has to be in neutral Spain." One of his thin smiles flashed. "I had the corporal install an Automatic Direction Finder in the L-5."

No one had thought it useful to review the consulate's Baedeker travel guide for Spain. It gave the historic town of Tarifa across the Strait only one page; Spain had too many other castles. Even though in year AD 711 the medieval walled town had been the first point of the Moorish invasion from Africa to Europe. The Tarifa fortress remained in Arab hands until year AD 1295 when 'el Sancho de Bravo' retook the castle. Three years later, Arabs attacked again. Alonzo Perez de Gúzman, 'el Bueno', refused to surrender even when offered the life of his captured only son.

Never having received instrument training for flight in bad weather, Jernigan knew little about sophisticated navigation devices but was intrigued.

At the airport he examined the new ADF starting with the obvious. The radio's antenna was a copper wire that stretched from the 'Sentinel' cabin top to the vertical stabilizer. Even though the airframe was wood and doped fabric, it was insulated at both ends and looked O.K. The signal receiver installed in the tail looked much like any other black box. Never before having seen under any fuselage a loop that twisted, he assumed it was for navigation.

The Automatic Direction Finder's indicator dial with a control knob was newly mounted in the cockpit instrument panel. No technical manual with operating instructions had been provided. With the engine running at idle and not pushing the wheel chocks, he clicked the instrument 'on'. Twisting the knob took some time to find the same medium range frequency detected by Browne's corporal. With the frequency locked on, the cockpit dial's needle corresponded immediately, swung and pointed toward the station's bearing. He was startled to hear someone speak German like he was in his bedroom.

"Hot damn. That's it."

The windsock still flapped on its pole; he could see a rosy glow rising over the eastern horizon. Time to go.

On takeoff, he always felt a rush, a thrill with the look of everything below becoming smaller. This time in the air, climbing while banking into a turn he watched the ADF needle move in response to his turn. He stayed in the climbing turn until the needle swung around to zero degrees on the dial. Dead ahead was the station's location.

After leveling off at 700 feet, he found it difficult to keep the airplane's needle fixed on that German station's bearing. Almost immediately the needle had begun moving; pointing to the right of zero. Jernigan quickly reasoned that a strong east wind was blowing him sideways, off course, to the west. So he'd better turn into the wind.

He kept the needle centered on zero by crabbing sideways nine degrees to the right of his magnetic compass destination.

In no time he was over Tangier, over the Strait and rapidly approaching the Spanish coast. Ahead loomed a small harbor and a several streets with buildings nestled at the base of a mountain. Suddenly he saw the needle jiggle. He knew he must be close, almost there. He throttled back. In a few seconds the needle swung around to read 180 degrees.

He grunted. "That's the radio. But where exactly was it?"

He flew in a wide circle, watching and following the needle's movements. At first there was not much to see outside the cockpit in the mist of early dawn. The mountain's slope to the harbor was forested with trees and scrub and . . . what's that? He flew closer; the ADF needle became erratic, again swung 180 degrees. He banked sharply and looking down in the turn had a clear view of a large stone fortress in a clearing. Must be it. He saw two figures on the rampart looking up. Time to leave.

Mission accomplished.

Within the hour after the American L-5's departure from Tangier, Abwehr General Auer's agent had made a routine report. It was received in Casablanca, filed and forgotten.

In Tangier, Daoud, sitting at a Café de Paris sidewalk table with a glass of mint tea, saw it pass overhead. He called long distance from a certain public telephone booth. When SS Major Rolf Niedermayer heard, then saw, the military aircraft circling his Tarifa, Spain fortress, he sent a coded telex to his SS controller in Paris.

In Paris, that telex was deemed important.

After Hitler invaded Russia, Himmler and his SS protégé General were not so assured of the war's out-come as was Hitler. Nor did they believe the Wehrmacht or Kriegsmarine intelligence that the American invasion target was Dakar, even though Admiral Doënitz had diverted to the south many of his submarines. The telex was deemed important because Himmler and Schellenberg, convinced the Allied fleet was coming to the Strait, had placed a transmitter in Spain for a future alert. They also had installed a Top Secret device that could eliminate any invading fleet.

Chapter Twenty Five

Capt. Browne arrived at the pension to pickup Jernigan for the prearranged early morning briefing.

Jack, in the small room adjacent to the kitchen, was savoring his arabica black coffee after wolfing down orange juice and a croissant as well as a baguette with goat cheese.

"Let's go," Browne said. "He'll be waiting."

Red-eyed and weary, Lieutenant Colonel Eddy focused on his Lieutenant's account of finding the transmitter location. Even though the night had been spent in the Minza office, coding responses to Donovan's antsy concerns and in addition coordinating vice-consul activities, his questions were succinct. Satisfied with answers, he rubbed his eyes and said, "Well done. Now on to what we need to do."

Eddy frowned a few moments in further thought then ordered Capt. Browne to create and head a commando squad to take out the German radio. Lieutenant Jernigan would lead the way. Unresolved was how to transport all the necessary OSS personnel and equipment.

He listened to Browne comment that swimming the Strait was impossible. Nor could so many personnel with gear be concealed in the small trawler. Besides, the

Tarana would have to dock somewhere, be conspicuous. A niggling thought in Eddy's mind moreover, was that a military force could be considered a foreign invasion of neutral Spain.

Jernigan spoke up, mentioned his recent covert action training and volunteered to go it alone. Colonel Eddy asked him how he planned to get there. He suggested a way and for lack of a better alternative, Eddy reluctantly consented.

Jernigan was elated – someone like him who liked to venture alone into wilderness to chip rocks was not a team player.

Eddy then briefed him on using one of his paid informers in the town, a man who could be of some assistance.

As Browne left, Eddy called to Jernigan: "Wait a minute. Your Colt with extra clip weighs well over three pounds. That's too heavy and cumber-some for this job."

Once again, he dug into his bottom drawer and took out another OSS weapon, the new M1942 Liberator with suppressor. It was a single-shot, .45-caliber pistol designed for very close range – just a handle, a short barrel that loaded through the muzzle and a trigger. Smaller than a derringer, the pistol was more powerful within six feet.

He also gave him a cyanide pill to crunch alongside his tongue.

Just in case.

He had been introduced only as JJ.

Wearing civilian clothing with borrowed paratrooper boots, a parachute and his ditty bag strapped across his chest, he stood tense and braced at the open door. Along with midshipmen at the Pensacola Naval Air Station he had received instruction but never actually jumped from a plane. Too soon the RAF Lancaster mail and supply plane that regularly transported diplomatic pouches from Gibraltar to London slowed, lost altitude and the navigator yelled, "Go Yank, Go!"

The unmarked white silk parachute blossomed. In less than two minutes, JJ made a tumbled landing on a moonlit slope above the Spanish town. For a moment he lay still, breathing rapidly and listening, then unbuckled and rolled up the parachute with its paratrooper harness. He was pushing it under bushes when he heard a twig snap. He pulled out his gun and stood alert behind an olive tree.

Scanning the darkened countryside, he saw nothing. Below, a dog barked, a small animal scuttled through brush.

Soon JJ heard a voice whisper: *"Aqui,* here *señor.* No shoot."

A bulky figure in a rumpled suit appeared and said: "Toreador."

JJ studied him while replying,: "Matador."

During the halting conversation that followed, JJ learned his contact was an anti-fascist, anti-Franco tribal Basque who loved America and had a cousin in Miami. The elderly man was hardly a combatant, worse, had never been inside Gúzman Castle.

Apologetic, he mentioned few foreign tourists would drive or ride a bus over the poor roads of the Costa de la Luz just to visit this fortress. Those who ventured into

Franco's civil-war-torn country would rather experience the Alhambra, stay in a Parador in Toledo or see the el Greco and Velazquez paintings in Madrid's Prado Museum.

More to the point, he knew nothing about the number and location of German guards. He thought his only obligation was to help JJ escape afterward. JJ spat on the hard ground.

The massive crumbling fortress was embedded as part of the town wall. On its moonlit side, he studied an archway door big enough for a carriage or two horsemen abreast. Behind and above soared a castellated citadel. All looked impregnable. Crouching, JJ worked his way around to the dark side of the outer wall that straggled uphill and enclosed what must be the citadel's forecourt. Thirty foot high it was a mixture of irregular stones, brick and limestone dug out of the bay offshore.

When he heard boot studs overhead, he timed the guard's pacing. Soon satisfied, he swung a small bronze grappling hook in a circle, let fly. Feeling the hook stick in rock, he hoisted himself up the rope. He dropped down the wall's other side and ran across the open space toward the citadel, pausing only to get his bearings. All was quiet. Nearby a guard lounged before the citadel's door.

This is *it*, he thought, then swallowed and sprinted.

Startled, the guard raised his submachine gun but before he could see to fire, the Liberator's bullet tore through his throat and out the spine. JJ caught his MP-40 Schmeisser with its forty round magazine before it could clatter onto the stone floor.

He didn't want to think about his killing a man. He concentrated on reloading the single-shot pistol by using the wood stick to pry out the spent casing and pushing another bullet into the muzzle. He dragged the body away then opened the door.

Inside was a large hall whose bare walls once held stacked muskets, helmets and breastplates; on the flagstone floor remained the original trestle table with benches. After listening, and hearing only silence, he started up the steep, narrow stone stairs that were illuminated by kerosene lanterns, his rubber-soled Keds canvas shoes making no sound. He stopped, dropped to his knees, and eyes level with the landing, saw two doors.

Through the open one, he could see two men playing cards at a table. He crept higher. At the next landing two doors showed no light at their sill, but a third did. Right hand holding the Schmeisser, JJ tiptoed toward the light, turned the doorknob and stepped in.

Seated at a table, a German soldier in uniform was tuning a radio. "*Ya? Vas iste,*" the soldier said without turning to look.

JJ walked forward, stood behind the soldier and smacked the base of his skull with the butt of the Schmeisser. JJ waited a moment, the compact sub machine gun held at the ready. No one came. He turned back to the transmitter. It had a sturdy, efficient-looking design. A shame, he thought and fired a burst. The radio exploded in a shower of sparks, metal, wires and Bakelite knobs. He felt exuberant with all that firepower, a job well done. Until he wondered, how am I going to get out?

He turned to the open door. A German Major stood there buttoning his jacket and taking in the scene.

JJ saw the Iron Cross pinned to his uniform and hanging around his neck the Knight's Cross – obviously this was a hardened combat officer.

JJ said: "Tell your men below to stay put. Then you sit down, here." He motioned with the gun.

The Major looked back and shouted something, came into the room. He pushed the unconscious soldier into a heap on the floor and sat down with a sardonic grin.

JJ lowered the Schmeisser.

The Major motioned: "A cigarette?"

JJ nodded.

The Major slowly took a shiny slender case six inches long from the side pocket of his jacket. He had his thumb on what appeared to be a seal or insignia in the top. "This will interest you," and his other hand lifted out from its side a short rod.

JJ came closer for a better look.

"Antenna," said the Major, eyes fixed on JJ's. "If I push this button, my device will send a signal to sonobuoys in the entrance to the Strait. These will listen for ship engines and screws. Then, its fuses will detonate and a large minefield under water will rise. Each mine contains a powerful explosive, sufficient on contact to blow a hole in your thickest warship hull." He stood up. "Put down the Schmeisser."

JJ dropped the submachine gun.

"Now *you* sit down."

JJ sighed. He sat on the chair and slumped low in obvious defeat. When he straightened up the Liberator was out of his thick sock and the Major had a red- rimmed hole between the eyes.

JJ carefully grasped the silver case, lowered the antenna and put the device into his bag. Then he picked up the Schmeisser and ran to the landing. But as he reached the stairs a hailstorm of bullets near him chipped stones from the wall. He dropped to the floor. More bullets went whining past as prone, he fumbled within his bag, yanked the pin from a grenade, threw and hugged the floor as shrapnel flew everywhere.

Downstairs in the main hall, he paused, heard no sounds. He opened the citadel door and ran a zigzag pattern to the wall's entrance; bullets from another forecourt guard followed him with a spray of flagstone chunks splattering in the air. JJ dropped into a shoulder roll and emptied the Schmeisser. The guard swayed, sagged to the ground.

Outside the wall and not seeing anyone, JJ hurried down hill. At the road, a figure leaned out the open side of an ancient truck, its engine clanking.

"*Aqui!*" shouted Toreador.

"For God's sake," muttered JJ, pushing the Basque aside and grabbing the cracked steering wheel himself. When he tried shifting gears, the grinding was horrendous. Must go the other way, he realized, and got the truck moving. There was only one road in or out of town.

With the engine sometimes backfiring, he had the truck chugging slowly up the mountain. There was no rearview mirror but on a switchback he could see below and coming up fast a kübelwagen.

Two soldiers in it fired. He mashed the accelerator pedal to the floor, twisted the wheels around an uphill curve. The mountain squeezed the narrow road on one side and on the other the sheer precipice fell far below to a rock strewn stream. The truck skidded on the pavement around the next curve and again he looked back.

Behind, the jeep-like military vehicle was less than three hundred yards and gaining. JJ steered around the mountain's next outcrop, backed up and positioned the truck with its tailgate jammed against rock. Pushing the Basque out the truck's far side, he followed just in time as the Nazis vehicle came roaring around toward them.

Brakes squealed; impact pushed the truck aside dislodging rocks. The Nazi green-painted vehicle bounced off the truck, skidded sideways off the road, rolled over and over down to the stream far below.

Chapter Twenty Six

Two days later, Jernigan sat in the back seat of a tiny Fiat as a German agent drove the potholed, weed-filled track south toward the fishing village of Asilah.

He had previously met with the Colonel at the Minza office, where Eddy reviewed the Roosevelt situation in every detail. There was no other OSS option; no turning back. Admittedly desperate, the bombing ploy must proceed.

Jernigan still thought the operation had too many unknowns and dared venture one more time that the most direct approach was for him to shoot any Nazi bringing the aircraft. By the time a replacement pilot was found Roosevelt would be gone and safe.

Eddy had reflected only an instant before ordering: "You do the mission as planned."

"Yes Sir."

Lieutenant Jernigan not surprised, silently watched Colonel Eddy lean over his deep drawer again and this time pull out a lightweight Browning semiautomatic. JJ holstered it inside his thick sock.

Now, nearing the outskirts of Asilah, Jernigan was surprised to see one of the French Delowite 520 aircraft on a small grass strip. He wanted a better look at the late model fighter – but the driver ignored him and continued toward the shore where he stopped near a moored seaplane.

A thug with a machine pistol dangling at his side climbed out of the cockpit's rear seat. Surprised again, Jernigan saw following him a tall, dark-haired man whose casual stance on one of the floats looked familiar. Goosen. He had dyed his hair.

"So," the Dutchman rasped with his usual grin. "Old friends meet again." This time his grin looked malicious, his eyes hard enough to slice diamonds. "You know where Roosevelt is staying. That foolish President still thinks he will see his fleet enter the Strait, as though passing in Review."

With the thug's Schnell Feuer Mauser pointed at him and Goosen available as a last resort pilot, any opportunity to use the Browning vanished. Teeth gritted, Jernigan eyed the big high-wing seaplane. He noted the aircraft sporting French markings was equipped with three machine guns lacking cartridge belts.

Goosen became all business; spoke as one pilot to another. "You won't have a problem. Flew her here myself, very maneuverable. I'm sure you understand why it is better not to use our German Stuka – the best dive bomber."

Jernigan said nothing; stood looking grim-faced.

"This dive bomber can do the job. It's from the French Escadrille Aeronautique Navale." He patted the cowling where twelve cylinders purred at idle. "Max speed with a Hispano-Suiza engine is one hundred sixty-seven miles per hour. The tank in the left float is half full, more than enough."

He pointed to the monstrous bomb slung between the floats then at two toggle switches on a small metal box in the cockpit. "Simple. First switch arms the bomb's detonator, second releases the bomb. The money is under the seat. She is all yours. *Bon chance,*" and he stepped onto the wharf and strode away.

"Yeah, good luck," Jernigan, muttered then laughed with a sudden thought. Yes, the bomber was all his. And he was going to crash her straight into the water with the bomb unarmed. He might not survive but Goosen would never get another plane and bomb in time.

Seated, he was studying the instrument panel when he heard the screech of brakes.

Looking toward the shore he saw the familiar big Mercedes skid to a stop fifty feet away. Moments later another thug was pulling April out of the car, grasping her by the nape of her neck. Her wrists were tied with rope.

"What the – "

April shouted: "These apes think you need a little pressure. Never mind me."

Jernigan unbuckled, began climbing out of the cockpit. "I'm coming."

"No." She screamed. "Don't. Do whatever you have to do."

Damn it. These guys are smart, he thought. Now what will I do? He shouted back: "I'm sorry, truly sorry."

He took a deep breath. "You're their hostage; insurance that I won't just crash this plane or fly away with their money. I'm supposed to bomb the Consulate with Roosevelt in it."

Open mouthed, April twisted in the German's grasp to stare. "I can't believe – I don't believe you."

He forced a smile with a wave goodbye; wished he could tell her it was all part of a plan . . . everything except now her capture. He buckled up again and signaled the thug to release the mooring rope.

He taxied at length, getting the feel of controls and ocean wave action on the floats until he thought, now or never, and applied full power.

When the slamming of metal on waves became the smoothness of air, he headed north-northeast, gained altitude to a thousand feet. During climb-out he checked again the instruments and switches. He leaned closer to read a small brass label: Fume. Must mean smoke he thought. Should have known, same as our Navy. He knew cruisers catapulted seaplanes from the aft deck to serve as scout dive-bombers; they also smoke-screened fleets from enemy cannon.

After leveling off, Jernigan squirmed, pulled the manilla envelope from underneath his seat. Inside, the bundle of U.S. one thousand dollar bills was secured with a red rubber band. After riffling the tight pack like a deck of cards, he slid open the small rectangular window that pilots used to talk to ground crew. Pulling off the band, taking one greenback, he felt it crisp between his fingers. "Freshly printed," he grunted and pushed the large pack through the opening, out into the slipstream. Immediately he banked and circled to watch the counterfeit notes flutter away like confetti.

Wanting time to think, he flew off course, turning east toward the snow-capped Atlas Mountains, thinking hard about his options. None looked good. Everything had changed with April's capture. Jaws set, he turned again, northwest with Tangier visible ahead. He would dump the bomb somewhere, then put this sucker into Tangier Bay where he would jump out. Then he'd somehow rescue April with the Browning.

By habit he craned his neck and did a thorough scan of the sky looking for any other aircraft in his airspace. There was. At four o'clock high.

He used aileron to lift the starboard wing while pushing opposite rudder to hold course and gazed upward. That French fighter was making a lazy circle overhead. Goosen. In a flash he realized if he dumped the bomb the bastard would strafe, machine-gun him. Same thing if he didn't do the bombing.

Jernigan flew on automatically while again rethinking his plan. Nothing seemed doable, let alone perfect. Descending to five hundred feet and heading for the American Consulate at the old city wall, he wished this airplane had a plastic bubble for a better view of Goosen's position.

At three hundred feet the target building loomed large, passed underneath; the harbor came fast. Moored at that same pier used by Germans he saw a large yacht. A large swastika flag fluttered at the stern. Ah ha! Target of Opportunity.

He flicked the toggle switch arming the bomb while circling to come around on the tail of Auer's yacht. He aimed at the flag, swooped almost to the deck, released the bomb.

The explosion blasted skyward rocking the seaplane. Jernigan struggled with the controls. Blackened splinters of wood, shards of glass and large pieces of metal smacked against the floats, wing and fuselage.

Tracer bullets suddenly formed two parallel lines of small sizzling waterspouts in the water.

Well, now for some real action, he thought. He slipped the seaplane sideways from the tracers. The French fighter, coming down fast, overshot and zoomed up to come around again.

The slow seaplane, dodging and weaving like a punch-drunk boxer, flew out of the curved harbor, across the bay and headed for the rocky promontory facing Gibraltar.

Jernigan was hoping a patrolling spitfire would show up like the cavalry always did in movies. But this was no Western and Goosen was again on his tail. The Malabata lighthouse loomed huge and tall straight ahead. Reaching it, he banked so steeply the gyroscope's artificial horizon went vertical, tumbled. Around the tower he flew close like at a Reno Air Race pylon. Goosen followed in the fighter, his turn tight too. He fired a short burst. That's when Jack groped for, found and flipped the toggle.

The right hand float spewed dense black smoke like a crop duster.

Goosen tried to turn away. His left wing, down to circle the lighthouse, shot up. Its tip scraped the brick tower. The fighter slewed around and down onto the promontory, skidded, struck the rock and erupted in a ball of flame.

"Hot damn!" Jernigan shouted. He hadn't had so much excitement since trying that carrier landing.

His face was beaded with sweat.

Chapter Twenty Seven

At the pension Omar Khayyam Jack sat down and the bed squeaked.

April's eyes fluttered open. She smiled and one arm held open the covers. For a moment he stood motionless, still amazed she was here, gaping at her curvaceous body, happy.

"Hurry. I'm shivering."

But when he held her in tight embrace she was very warm.

Afterward she whispered: "Let's celebrate."

"Celebrate what?"

"My escape, dummy."

Fast and without emotion, she told him what had happened.

"Incredible," he whispered and kissed her. "It's hard to believe . . . that part where, with your wrists still tied, you pulled the Browning out of your cleavage . . . and shot the ape in the throat?"

April frowned. "Good thing Eddy's OSS pistol didn't have a hammer. How embarrassing if it had caught and snagged my brassiere."

Jack laughed; leaning on one elbow he changed the subject. "What's new at the spy works?"

"My ruse worked."

Jack stretched to the bedside table, pulled a cigarette from the pack. "I know you're a busy girl. What ruse?"

"A deception. I wrote and encrypted a false American message from our Colonel, one that fooled German intelligence into passing it on to Hitler."

"Are you sure? How do you know Hitler got it?" He gave her his cigarette and reached for another.

"Would you believe I deciphered his order to Admiral Doënitz? All submarines were to go from the Strait to the Atlantic, south and east of the Azores. Those subs went to intercept our fleet going to Dakar."

Jack, thinking she looked bushed, said: "You've been working too hard, long hours too. Our Colonel certainly owes you. Tell you what we'll do. The MIDWAY radio is at his villa. We can listen in on what's happening with the invasion. Eddy won't be there; he and Browne went to Commander O'Brien's office in the Gibraltar Consulate."

"Eisenhower is there too, with top brass at the Rock hotel."

"How do you know?"

April giggled. "Browne wanted a deception. So I chit-chatted with my peer in London, said Ike was in Tangier watching Bob Hope and Bing Crosby in the 'Road to Morocco' movie."

"Clever," your figuring the Germans would intercept.

192

The Tangier Option

Watching smoke float upward, remembering the B-24 landing at that tight little airstrip, Jack was thinking Ike's pilot has it easy. Gibraltar's runway is now a broad mile-long; built out over the bay with rubble from all that tunneling.

"How do we get in? To the villa – "

"Mohammad knows me."

It was almost sunrise over the villa on the Old Mountain.

Jack knew better than use the library that Eddy had converted to his Naval office. But up in the Eagles Nest, he took the thirty-pound radio and battery out of a suitcase. "Here's your MIDWAY radio," he said, unfolding a coil of aerial wire. "Maybe I can find the ship-to-ship frequency."

"Let's see what's in the fridge." April found champagne and poured two glasses. She sipped hers, stretched out on a banquette while he fiddled with several frequencies.

Invasion hour H-0620 arrived just as Jack said: "I've got it."

April joined him and both hovered over the radio, listening to the ship-to-ship frequency announce: "Now hear this. Now hear this: BATTER UP, BATTER UP."

Two minutes later came the command: "PLAY BALL!"

Those aboard ships saw a star shell bursting high that illuminated the Moroccan beach and scattered whitecaps near the shore.

At the villa Jack grabbed April by the waist and they danced around the small space until she whispered in his ear: "See what else you can get on the radio while I open

193

another bottle." She added, "Might just as well return two bottles to our Colonel instead of just one."

Within minutes, Jack had tuned in a German voice: "*Achtung, achtung, achtung. Ein amerikanisches kraftsheer ist auf den nordwest Kuste Africas gelandet.*"

April glanced at Jack and loosely translated. "He's saying American boats have landed."

Jack remembered the French defenses, hoped they weren't giving our guys a hard time but said nothing to April.

Seeking something else, April returned to the set, bent over Jack and slowly twisted the tuning knob. She was surprised to hear a gramophone recording of President Roosevelt in his prep school French repeating over and over: "*Allo — Franklin arrivé, Allo — Franklin arrivé.*" The transmitter then relayed the Marseillaise and the Star Spangled Banner.

After standing in a stiff brace, Jack sprawled in an upholstered chair. "Inspiring anthem, but glad I don't have to sing it."

April laughed. "Franklin is the code word to let the French resistance fighters in Morocco know that Roosevelt's voice is for real."

Jack leaned over April who had again stretched out on a long banquette, kissed her forehead.

She pouted. "That's nice. Friendly, I suppose."

Jack sat down in the leather chair beside her. "I'm going to ask Colonel Eddy for a transfer."

She smiled. "Every military man wants that at some time or other."

"I mean it."

April sat up abruptly, spilling half the champagne in her lap. "Don't joke."

"Look at it this way. My cover is blown. By now, the whole town knows I'm a double agent. My usefulness as an assistant Navy attaché . . . that's over."

Frowning, she studied his somber face. After a pause, she said: "You mean it don't you. Will Eddy agree?"

"I figure I've got two options." He avoided looking at her. "Did you know the Navy advanced flight trainer, the NVG, is the same as the Army Air Corps AT-6? I have a couple hundred hours in the AT-6, shouldn't that count for something? Maybe I could reactivate my army commission, be assigned to an Air Corps fighter squadron."

April gulped the remaining champagne from her glass; rose and headed for the fridge to get another refill. She hoped bubbles would calm her.

Jack called out after her: "You don't like that option. Neither do I. How about this one: Admiral Hewitt is sitting out there, offshore Casablanca. I go to Eddy and ask our Marine Colonel to talk to Hewitt's Executive Officer, put in a good word for me. He could get the XO to talk to Hewitt, help arrange my transfer to the fleet. Maybe I could fly a scout plane off a cruiser, or pilot a flying boat . . . I have some experience with a seaplane, you know." His chuckle was forced.

She turned away and stared out the window, seeing nothing, feeling drained. Her voice was flat. "What makes you think the Admiral would be interested?"

Jack grinned. "I hadn't mentioned it, but the other day Colonel Eddy told me my fitness report would be 4-0. That's tops, you know. What's more, he put in my file a copy of Hewitt's letter to him giving a 'Well Done' on my recon of the French coastal defenses. My maps and reports had been distributed to naval and army commanders."

Blinking back tears, April was thinking this is like a Hollywood movie where the mistress gets kissed off. She took a deep breath, said instead. "I hope you get what you want." She picked up her purse.

Jack went to her; she was trembling. He put his hands on her shoulders, looked at the tears forming, pulled her close. He whispered in her ear: "Honey, I'll tell you what I really want – marry me."

They drank a toast to a long future together.

EPILOGUE

*The Torch Operation Plan had three parts:

1. Eastern Naval Task Force whose mission was to capture Algiers shipped out of the Firth of Clyde, Scotland, October 22. Commanded by RADM Sir H. M. Burroughs RN with Eastern Assault Force Major General C. W. Ryder, USA, commanding 22,000 British and 60,000 American troops. The fleet consisted of 46 cargo vessels escorted by 18 warships. Astern of this convoy was a second flotilla of 39 transports.

2. Center Naval Task Force whose mission was to capture Oran in Algeria, departed Rosneath, Scotland October 23. Commodore Thomas Trowbridge RN commanding 19,870 officers and men embarked on twelve transports, four of which were assault transports and three, cargo vessels.

3. Western Task Force (TF34, entirely American) whose mission was to capture Atlantic Ocean coastal installations in Morocco, stood out of Hampton Roads, Virginia at 8:00 A. M. October 23, RADM Admiral Hewitt commanding. The Military force consisted of U.S. Army 9th Infantry

Division from Fort Bragg, NC, 35,000 troops, 250 tanks commanded by General George S. Patton and a battalion of paratroopers who made the first combat jump of the war. This force was divided into three groups according to target.

The Northern Attack Group (Admiral Kelly) to land General Truscott with 9,000 soldiers at the mouth of the Sebou River to take the airport at Port Lyautey where 168 French aircraft were operational; the Center Attack Group (Captain Emmet) to Place General Anderson with 19,000 soldiers on beaches at Fedala, 15 miles North of Casablanca; the Southern Attack Group (Admiral L. Davison) to land General Harmon with 6500 soldiers and 125 tanks at the harbor of Safi, 140 miles south of Casablanca. The Casablanca harbor was considered suicidal because of powerful shore batteries.

Torch Air Group, whose mission was to assist the Northern Attack Group's capture of Port Lyautey and to use its airport as a base, was commanded by RADM Admiral Ernest D. McWhorter aboard the carrier USS Ranger. His flotilla included one light cruiser, one oilier, nine screening destroyers and the four "Sangamon" Class escort carriers just out of the yards. Carried were 26 Grumman Avenger torpedo bombers, 36 Douglas Dauntless dive-bombers and 108 Wildcat fighters. Also ferried were 76 U.S. Army P-40's to be catapulted and based at the Casablanca aerodrome soon as it was captured.

Tangier Gazette
November 9, 1942.

The Gazette was printed in BLUE, the masthead in RED. The price: 1 franc. Page 1, in Spanish: "Fuerzas Americas Desembarcos en varios puntos de las costas Mediterranean y atlantica del Africa del Norte ancesa. El General Eisenhower manda el cuerpo expedicionario Americana." The front page showed large pictures of Roosevelt and Eisenhower.

Page 2: A small box ad with a drawing of a hand advertised Professor S. Elazar who looked at the lines of your hands to reveal the future.

Tangier Gazette
November 10, 1942.

The front page again pictured Roosevelt and a smiling Eisenhower together.

Pg. 3: "The British Red Cross Society in Tangier announces a Grand Bazaar to be held on Thursday, 19 November at the Hotel Villa de France and requests contributions. A naval engagement off Casablanca was crowned with success for the Allies. Fighting has taken place at Safi and Fedala. According to Radio Tanger the Rabat aerodrome has been evacuated by French forces . . . U.S. forces have landed at Port Lyautey."

Pg. 4 Advertisements: New Swedish merchandise- electric cooking ranges with one or two holes; a large choice of paper sanitary articles.

The OSS in Tangier that Radio Berlin had described as: "Fifty professors, twenty monkeys, ten goats, twelve guinea pigs and a staff of Jewish scribblers," had well done its job of disinformation. Hitler had sent the German Atlantic Fleet with thirty submarines directed by the Kriegsmarine to a position in the Azores off shore Dakar, Africa. The remaining submarine wolfpack and motor torpedo boats attacked RADM C.N. Reyne 's British convoy going north along the Atlantic seaboard of Africa. These were all empty ships sacrificed in Operation TORCH.

On the night of November 3, British Covering Force H, consisting of three battleships, two aircraft carriers, three cruisers and seventeen destroyers entered the Strait. Its crucial mission was to defend Torch landings against German, Italian and Vichy Mediterranean fleets.

When the Abwehr radio in Lisbon reported a large British fleet rounding Portugal on its way to the Strait of Gibraltar, Hitler was not perturbed. He shrugged, "Another supply convoy coming to Malta. Our Eastern Mediterranean German and Italian submarines will sink three quarters of the vessels. Same as last time."

On November 7 the Tangier Chargé d'Affaires ad interim forwarded a letter from President Roosevelt to Resident General Auguste Noguès officially announcing the impending invasion and requesting non-intervention by Vichy French forces. Hand carried by a junior officer, only a Navy lieutenant, arrogant General Noguès refused that critical day to open the letter.

That day at 0200 hours, General Antoine Bethcourt, Commander Casablanca Division, awakened French General Noguès with news that Americans would be landing on Moroccan beaches before dawn. He further announced that he had assumed military command of the French Protectorate in order to welcome the American forces. Infuriated, Noguès immediately had him arrested tried, convicted and sentenced to execution for treason. Late that morning Noguès issued the order for all French forces to resist the Americans.

The radio Duty Officer at the German Armistice Commission in Casablanca heard President Roosevelt's broadcast. He alerted General von Wulish who that afternoon called on Noguès to bid farewell. With tears in his eyes, he said: "This is the greatest setback to Germany since 1918. The Americans will take Rommel in the rear, we shall be expelled from all Africa."

Just before sunrise November 7 at 0620 hours, the battle for Fedala-Port Lyautey was on.

There was a huge difference between the Plan and the Operations. In darkness, officers did not know the relative positions of boats. Troops carrying heavy loads of rifles plus equipments moved slowly from transport vessels to landing craft. Some transports failed to arrive at designated locations on time. Inexperience, attempting to steer by the star Sirius and rocky ledges with landing on a falling tide caused large losses of landing boats.

Experienced French pilots in Dewoitine fighters fought pilots in aircraft of the Ranger and Escort Carriers. Lt. Commander Booth's Red Ripper Squadron proved superior in dogfight tactics as well as strafing ground targets in support of troops.

French troops put up a stiff resistance, counter attacking at the vital airstrip at Port Lyautey. There, handicapped by confusion, brief training and lack of combat experience, U.S. Coast Guardsmen and soldiers persevered with courage and intelligence.

At Casablanca harbor, none of the officers of the French battleship *Jean Bart* who opened fire with their antiaircraft and 15 inch guns knew what they were firing at – American or German warships? Their battleship became a smoking hulk.

An Allied column of troops headed for Tunisia and General Rommel.

A patriotic Frenchman in Algeria assassinated Admiral Darlan who had played both sides: Axis and Allied.

Admiral Canaris was executed along with Colonel Klaus von Stauffenberg and other conspirators who attempted to assassinate Hitler in his Wolf's Lair, near Rastenberg, deep in the east Prussian forest.

General Noguès was tried by the Free French, convicted and sentenced to exile in Portugal.

The OSS became much more professional, bureaucratic and, after the war, morphed into the Central Intelligence Agency.

TORCH AIR GROUP IN COMBAT

	Ranger	Santee	Survanee	Sangamon
Sorties	446	144	255	83
Planes Lost				
F4F-4	12	10	3	0
SBD-3	3	4	0	2
TBF-1	0	7	2	1

OPERATION TORCH CASUALTIES MOROCCO

American:
- Killed: 531
- Wounded: 1,054
- Missing: 237

French:
- Killed: 651
- Wounded: 553
- Missing: 0

Total: 3,026

*Adapted from public sources and Morrison, Samuel Eliot, *Operations in North Africa Waters, October 1942-June 1943; Vol. II. History of U.S. naval operations in WWII, Boston, 1947.*

GLOSSARY

Abwehr	Army Intelligence Branch (German)
Allah	God
Baraka	Blessing, luck, fortune
BuPers	Bureau of Naval Personnel
CAVU	Ceiling and visibility unlimited
DC	Washington, D.C.
DG	Director General
Fantasia	Festival, display of horsemanship
FNP	Former naval person
Fondouk	Bazaar, former caravan lodgings
G-2	Military Intelligence Division (War Department)
Grand Socco	Main plaza
Hammam	Public bath
Hijab	Woman's head scarf
Jellaba	Long outer garment
Jihad	Personal goal, holy war
Kaftan	Long cotton garment, caftan
Kasbah	Fortress, citadel, Casbah
Kif	Hemp, marijuana, hashish
Koubba	Domed shrine, Kubba
LSO	Landing signal officer
Marabout	Holy warrior, ascetic

Medina	Downtown, old city core
MI.6	Military covert intelligence (British)
MSL	Mean sea level
Muezzin	Arabic prayer announcer
ONI	Office of Naval Intelligence
OSS	Office of Strategic Services
POTUS	President of the United States
RAF	Royal Air Force
Schnell Feuer	Rapid fire
SIS	Secret Intelligence Service (British)
SOE	Special Operations Executive (British)
Souk	Marketplace

Other trade books published by Ethos Publishing:

Mustache Try-On Book (hard cover)
The Free Woman
Museums of Jordan: A Directory
Flicker in Morocco (forthcoming novel)
The Maya Option (forthcoming novel)